Desire

www.chellebliss.com
CHELLE BLISS
USA TODAY BESTSELLING AUTHOR

Publisher © Chelle Bliss May 1, 2026
Edited by Lisa A. Hollett
Proofread by Read By Rose & Shelley Charlton
Cover Design © Chelle Bliss
Cover Photo © Wander Aguiar

MEN OF INKED SINNERS SERIES

Book 1 - Crave

Book 2 - Want

Book 3 - Need

Book 4 - Wish

Book 5 - Desire

Book 6 - Promise

To learn more please visit

menofinked.com/sinners

The Men of Inked Sinners series is also available in discreet paperback & hardcover editions

CHAPTER 1
MASON

THE BAR IS NEARLY EMPTY, the midday rush having ended an hour ago. We've been busier lately than we've been in months, but that's normal when the city starts to thaw from a long, cold winter.

I glance down the bar, seeing Zoey with her forehead pressed against the counter. "Are you okay?"

She waves me off, not even bothering to lift her head or look my way. "Fine. Fine."

Growing up with an older sister, I know fine doesn't mean what it says in the dictionary. "What can I do to help?"

"Nothing. I'm just panicking about wedding stuff."

We're a month out from the big day, and I've been tasked with being the best man. I was honored when Hunter asked me, but the reason I jumped at the role was that his sister is the maid of honor.

"Everything will get done."

Zoey groans as she pushes herself upright. "I know, but it's just so much. Remember when I say this… elope," she says, drawing out the word.

"Noted," I tell her as I wipe away a wet spot on the counter in front of me. "With a front-row seat to your wedding and Tate's, eloping sounds perfect."

"Do it in a tropical and exotic location too. Somewhere with sun and sand."

"Florida?"

Zoey rolls her eyes before she rubs her forehead like I'm giving her a headache. "I said exotic. Who thinks Florida is exotic?"

"I do." I smirk, knowing I'm annoying her, but at least she's focused on me and not the other shit that's been running through her head. "Where do you think Lizzy will want to get married?"

Zoey's arms fall to her sides as her eyes widen. "Mason," she whispers.

"What?" I busy myself with useless tasks, avoiding her gaze.

"If you yank this woman around…"

"I'm not. I wouldn't," I tell her honestly.

"She's going to be my sister-in-law and your cousin-in-law."

"Cousin-in-law is not a thing, Zo."

She closes the space between us and touches my arm, stopping me from cleaning the countertop. "Do you really like her?"

I finally meet her gaze, wanting her to know exactly

how I feel. "I've never liked anyone else as much as I like her."

She tightens her fingers around my arm. "Please don't break her heart. This isn't a game."

My eyes narrow as I stare down at my cousin. "My plan isn't to hurt her. It's to put a ring on that finger."

"She's a small-town girl," she says, like I'm clueless about Lizzy's life.

"I'm well aware of where she and Hunter come from. But she loves Chicago, and as soon as she sees it in the summer, she's going to jump at the chance to live here. Especially since Hunter and Amira live here."

"Could you live in a small town?" she asks me pointedly.

"Um, no."

"Then don't assume she'd want to live here for any reason. Even love might not be strong enough to change everything about your life."

"Would you have moved if Hunter asked?"

She stares back at me and blinks a few times. "I think so." Her voice lilts upward on the last word as if she isn't sure, but I know my cousin. She would follow that man to the ends of the earth.

The doors to the bar open, letting in a stream of sunshine, something we've been lacking for months. Lizzy steps inside, and with the light behind her, she looks more like an angel than a human being.

My breath catches in my lungs as I soak her in. Her dark hair billows over the shoulders of her jacket, which is pulled tight to keep out the chilled air. She has on a pair of boots that aren't sexy at all, but necessary with the slush that seems to be everywhere as the snow starts to melt. I can't make out the features of her face until she takes a few steps into the bar and out of the sunlight.

"Hey," Lizzy says with a giant smile on her beautiful face. "Sorry I'm late."

"I didn't even notice," Zoey tells her, but she's lying. She notices everything, and it's been made worse by the stress of her impending nuptials. "We're easy breezy."

I snort and earn myself a jab in the side from my cousin. "Liar," I whisper as I grimace through the throb from my battered ribs.

Lizzy weaves through the empty tables, making her way in our direction. Her green eyes move to me, rising at the corners as soon as her gaze meets mine. "Hey, Mason."

"Hey," I say with a chin lift and immediately regret it. That's how I greet friends, not the woman I'm hopelessly in love with.

I know. I know. I barely know her. She's been in my life for under a year, but that doesn't mean my feelings aren't real. I knew the moment I laid eyes on her that I wanted her, but after spending time with her, especially after Hunter was shot, I knew I wanted more... I wanted everything with her.

We've hung out every time she's come to town since then. I've always been a perfect gentleman.

Although everyone in the family thinks we're already sleeping together. I listened to my cousin's and my sister's advice—take it slow. Something I've never been good at, but with Lizzy, it's surprisingly easy. The distance makes it easier. If I had to see her every day and move at a snail's pace, I'd probably lose my mind.

"We going out tonight?" Lizzy asks me as she slides onto a stool opposite where Zoey and I stand behind the bar.

Zoey clears her throat, clearly unhappy at how close Lizzy and I have become.

"Of course. Do you know where you want to go?" I ask her, always trying to let her lead and be a gentleman.

"Anywhere you want. I'm yours."

I nearly choke on my own spit at her reply. Damn. I crave to hear her say those words but mean them in their entirety. Slow, Mason. Slow.

"I'll pick you up at eight."

"Wow. You two are going to burn the midnight oil," Zoey says, her gaze moving between Lizzy and me. "You sure you don't want to do something earlier?"

I turn my head to my cousin and stare at her. "When did you turn into an old person?"

She clears her throat, stretching her neck in a way that I know I hit a chord I didn't entirely mean to hit. "I'm not old."

"No, you're not, and neither are we." I turn my

attention back to Lizzy, soaking in the green of her eyes as she watches me. "You want to do earlier?"

Lizzy shakes her head, brushing a few strands away from her cheek. "Eight is perfect. We have a lot to do before then."

"Fuck," Zoey groans and crumples over, resting her head against the bar top again. "There's so much to do."

Lizzy's eyes widen, and she turns to me, looking for a rescue, or maybe it's more concern. "Don't worry. It'll all fall into place." Lizzy reaches forward, placing her hand on top of my cousin's. "We're all here to help."

"There's not enough time to do it all," Zoey says, her voice muffled by the wood. "It's going to be a failure."

Lizzy strokes Zoey's hand with her thumb as she tries to soothe her. "All that matters is that you and Hunter are there and say your vows. Everything else is extra. Do you want to cancel everything and just go to city hall?"

Zoey pulls up her head but not her entire body. She's overly dramatic lately, but that isn't surprising. "I can't. I don't want that."

Everyone in the family has a bit of drama llama in them, but when there's extreme pressure like planning a wedding, they get even worse. I can't wait for the entire thing to be over so I don't have to hear about it every day at work. Zoey has always been chill, but she's been a bundle of nerves for months now.

"Then we'll get it done, and it'll be perfect," Lizzy tells her, and her voice doesn't waver. Even I believe what she's saying, though I know the chance of something going wrong is high. It's inevitable. "Mason and I are here to make sure of it."

I want to say something, but I keep my mouth shut. I'm not setting foot in the wedding planning. I didn't do it with my sister Tate when she got married to Wylder, and I sure as hell am not about to do it with Zoey. I know my limits, and wedding planning falls far outside my scope.

When I don't say anything, Lizzy slices her eyes to mine. "Right, Mason?"

"Yeah, sure. Of course," I say, but my voice isn't as strong or sure as Lizzy's. "We're here for whatever you need."

I'll always support my cousin. Just like I would for anyone else in my family. But who wants me, a twentysomething-year-old man, helping to plan their wedding? The bachelor party—that, I could do, but everything else would only end in disappointment because there isn't a frilly, girlie bone in my body.

Zoey pushes herself upright again and tugs on the hem of her sweatshirt as she straightens. "Okay. I can do this. I just need a minute," she says before she stalks away and into the back room.

The entire time, my eyes are trained on Lizzy. I can see worry all over her face. I've been around her enough to be able to pick up on most of her emotions, especially with the shit we've been through in such a short time.

"That girl is going to stroke out," Lizzy says as soon as Zoey disappears.

I chuckle as I lean over the bar, getting closer to Lizzy. "She'll be all right because she has you."

"And you," Lizzy says and reaches out, playfully bopping my nose with her finger. "You have a more calming presence than you know."

I snatch her hand in my grip, wanting and needing to touch her in any way possible. "You're the only one who would say that, Lizzy."

"You're like a warm hug or a favorite blanket."

I don't know if I should be offended by the statement. I want to be more than that, but I also like that I'm something that someone—specifically Lizzy—would wrap around their body.

"Is that a good thing?" I ask her.

"A very good thing," she says with a smirk.

Have I kissed this woman? No. Do I plan to tonight? Hell yes. I can't go another minute without touching my lips to hers. There's slow and then there's torture, and I've solidly slid into the painful side of the timing spectrum over the last few months. I don't want to do anything to drive her away, but it's gotten ridiculous by this point.

Everyone already thinks we've slept together. Sure, she's crashed at my place a few times, but I've always been a gentleman. She is Hunter's sister after all, and the last thing I need is that man coming after me for any reason.

"I'm going to need a few drinks after an afternoon of wedding planning. I hope wherever we're going, there's going to be alcohol."

I give her a wink. "I got you, baby."

Her cheeks turn a shade of pink that reminds me of the roses my mother grows in her front yard. "Good."

"Okay. I'm ready," Zoey says, walking out of the back room and pulling on her coat. If I hadn't been in the room, I wouldn't have guessed she was having a meltdown a few minutes ago. "Let's do this."

"Good," Lizzy says, jumping off the stool like her ass is on fire. "You want me to drive?"

"Uh," Zoey mutters and shakes her head. "I don't think that's a good idea."

Neither do I, but I don't say those words out loud. Driving in Chicago isn't for the faint of heart. Besides dodging other drivers, you have to keep your eyes out for the taxi drivers, who are the real danger when the roads are busy. They're in a hurry, and they don't have time for traffic laws or turn signals.

"Good, because I like my car without dents," Lizzy says with a chuckle as she moves toward the end of the bar where Zoey is standing.

"Oh, we're still taking your car, though. I didn't bring mine today," Zoey tells her.

Lizzy sticks her hand in her pocket, fishes out her keys, and holds them up to Zoey. "I have faith in you."

Zoey's a shit driver. It's almost a running joke in the family. She's the last person I'd give my keys to and hope the car returns in the same condition she got it. But again, I don't say a word because I don't need them both giving me the stink eye.

"Well, that's one of us," Zoey says as she takes the keys from Lizzy's hands. "I'll be careful. Don't worry."

"She would've made a great taxi driver," I say before they head for the door.

"I'll take that as a compliment," Zoey replies, but she knows it's not, even if Lizzy doesn't.

"Pick me up at eight. Don't forget about me," Lizzy says as she pulls a pair of sunglasses out of her other pocket and slides them onto her face.

"You're impossible to forget," I tell her, and I don't think I've ever said anything so true in my entire life.

I get a wave from each of them before they disappear into the crisp air that has a hint of spring, even if it's missing the warmth.

"You got it bad," Marvin says, the man a regular at the bar for decades. He knew me when I was knee-high, and he's watched me grow up as I've watched him age. "Real bad."

"Another?" I ask, my gaze dipping to the nearly empty beer in front of him.

He pushes the glass forward, silently answering my question. "You datin' her yet?"

I shake my head as I grab his glass.

"What's taking you so long? I've watched you pant after that woman for months now. You're not usually so slow."

"Marv," I say, warning him to drop it before I cut him off when he's only had two.

"Time isn't infinite, kid. It runs out eventually. Don't waste too much time trying to be a gentleman. When the big guy upstairs decides it's your time, it's your time. You don't want to be gasping for your last breaths, regretting what could've been if you weren't such a pansy-ass to go after it."

"Geez, bud." I set the refilled glass down in front of him. "You should really write inspiration books."

He takes the beer, lifts it up, and tips it in my direction without spilling a drop. "Take it from an old man, go after what you want and don't waste a single minute."

As much as I want to write off Marv as a man who overconsumes alcohol and doesn't know very much about anything except beer, he is right.

Time isn't infinite, and if I don't go after what I want, Lizzy will slip through my hands. I won't go down that path. I am going to act, and it is going to be swift.

CHAPTER 2
LIZZY

"SO," Zoey says as she weaves through traffic like she has eyes around her entire head.

I grip the door as I press my toes into the bottoms of my boots, hoping she isn't going to get us killed. "So…" The words come out strangled as my life flashes before my eyes.

"Mason," she says.

I knew where this conversation was going before she said his name. I'm surprised we haven't had it earlier.

"What's going on there?" she asks.

I turn my head to the side and smile. Mason makes my toes curl. Not only is he handsome as hell, he's sweet too. But I wouldn't expect anything less when it comes to a Gallo.

I haven't known the family long, but there isn't a single member who isn't kind and warm. I've never felt so welcomed, not even with my own family. The Gallos took us in immediately, and now I look forward to coming to Chicago to see the people I consider mine, even if we don't share any blood.

"I like him." My voice is small, like I'm telling her a secret I haven't voiced to anyone else in the world and have barely admitted to myself.

"Do you like him like him or *like him like him*?"

"He gives me butterflies." I regret that little admission as soon as the words are out of my mouth.

Another thing I know about the family is there's no such thing as secrets. Hunter told me as much, and I've experienced the transparency with which they operate for months now.

"Girrrrrl," Zoey says, drawing out the word before she jerks the car to the side to switch lanes.

I nearly yelp in surprise and clutch my chest as I try to calm my racing heart. "Zo, babe, I kinda want to live to see another day," I tell her, hoping my words are sweet enough not to upset her, but also to let her know she's driving like a lunatic.

"Show no fear," she mutters. "I got you. Don't worry. I'm an expert Chicago driver."

"Okay," I whisper and curl my fingers around the door handle a little tighter as if it's somehow going to protect me from the force of smashing into another thousand-pound object.

"Your brother gives me butterflies too," she says, but I already know that. No one says yes to marrying a man who doesn't make their belly flutter. She carries on the conversation like we aren't defying death with each passing foot of roadway.

"Where are we headed first?" I ask, wanting to change the subject away from Mason and any feelings, even confusing ones, I have about him.

The pull I feel toward him is immense. I've tried for months to fight it, but my strength is starting to falter. If things go to shit, which, in all likelihood, they will, it could complicate my brother's life since Zoey is Mason's cousin.

I've never been a casual type of relationship girlie either. A few times, I've thought about giving it a go with Mason, but I'll end up with a broken heart, and I don't want that for me either.

"We're grabbing Lulu and then heading to the bakery first to taste cakes."

"Hunter didn't want to come?" I'm surprised. The man loves cake more than most people, and his sweet tooth is something that's turned my stomach a time or two in my life as he gorged himself on sugary candy.

"He said he didn't care which one I picked because he loves them all."

"Typical," I mumble. "The man even likes coconut cake." I shiver at the thought. There's something about that extra-sweet cake with shredded coconut that has my sensory issues working overtime.

"Ick."

"My thoughts exactly."

We turn a corner, the back end of the car fishtailing from a patch of ice that hasn't melted. My heart stutters in my chest as Zoey regains control of the car.

"Those are fun," she tells me with a quick glance.

I give her a tight smile, trying not to be a total shit in the pants, even though I'm wishing I could have an out-of-body experience right now instead of being trapped inside this car. Maybe I'll be lucky, and Lulu will drive us the rest of the way. She has to be a better driver than Zoey. I can't imagine many people worse.

"There she is," Zoey says, ticking her chin toward the woman standing on the side of the road, jumping up and down while waving her arms wildly.

I'd know Lulu anywhere, and Zoey too. They're beautiful woman who turn every head when they walk by. Between their pretty faces and perfect bodies…don't even get me started on their amazing boobs.

"Is she driving?"

"Uh, no," Zoey replies, killing all hopes that we are going to have a more stress-free ride to the bakery. Maybe I'll get lucky, and it'll be around the corner. It could happen, right?

Zoey slams on the brakes, swerving the car to the side, sliding to the curb like she's a character in a video game.

Lulu bounces toward the car, climbing in the back seat before I have a chance to take a deep breath. "Heyyyy," Lulu says, slamming the door as soon as she's fully inside.

"Hey, sissy. Ready to roll?" Zoey asks, turning her upper half around to look at her sister.

"You know it. I've been dreaming of this cake day. It's the best thing ever."

My head jerks as Lulu bumps the back of my seat. "You okay? You look a little pale."

"Fine. Fine," I whisper, but I can't find the energy to move or turn around to give her a smile.

"She's new to my driving," Zoey tells her sister as she turns back around and grips the steering wheel like the second half of the trip is going to be worse than the first.

Lulu laughs. "It's why I sit in the back. I feel like it's safer with her driving."

"I'm not that bad," Zoey tells her sister, looking at her in the rearview mirror.

"You are, though. Why do you think Dad gave up on teaching you? He said, and I quote, *She thinks it's a video game.*"

Zoey chuckles. "He's dramatic."

My fingers curl into fists as I fight the urge to jump out of the car and spare myself a grisly death.

"He's not dramatic enough," Lulu replies as she clicks her seat belt into place. "I'm ready. Let's go. I have cake to eat."

Thirty minutes and three near misses of other cars later, we're inside the bakery. I've never been so thankful to be out of a car in my entire life. I think my little niece Amira could drive more cautiously than Zoey. I'd put money on it.

"Anyone want to do drinks later?" Lulu asks as we sit at a table, waiting for the woman to bring out our first set of taste tests.

"I'm game, but this one has a date with Mason." Zoey pitches her thumb at me. "At eight. They're going to dinner."

"Ooh," Lulu whispers. "This is getting exciting."

"It's not a date," I say a little too quickly and crisply. "We're friends."

"He gives you butterflies," Zoey says.

Lulu's eyebrows rise. "No shit. Really?"

"Really," Zoey answers for me.

"Damn. I love that," Lulu replies.

I might as well not be here. They're talking around me and not to me. It's fine, though, because I don't want to talk about the huge crush I have on their cousin that will go absolutely nowhere. We live hundreds of miles apart. Nothing could come of whatever the attraction we have is. His life is here…in the big city, and mine is back home where no speed limit is over twenty-five miles per hour, and I have to drive a half hour to the nearest store.

"You two have hung out a lot," Lulu says to me, finally bringing me into the conversation.

"A few times."

"More than a few times, and butterflies is huge, babe. Huge." Lulu knocks my shoulder with hers. "My cousin is a good egg. Sometimes he's a dipshit, but that's because he has balls. For the most part, he's solid."

"He's just been showing me around some of the great food places here in the city. He says they're hidden gems that he doesn't like to share with anyone."

Lulu leans back, crossing her arms as she studies me. "He has butterflies too, then."

"Why do you say that?" I ask. "It's been mostly pizza and beer."

"Because I've never seen Mason take anyone to his hidden gems. No one but you."

I make a little noise, but I have nothing to say to that.

"Did you two sleep together yet?" she asks.

I'm only mildly stunned by the question. Again, the Gallos are oversharers, and the topics are not always appropriate.

"No," I reply as I pick at the red polish that I somehow got on the skin of my index finger.

Lulu gasps. "No?"

I shake my head. "We're friends."

"Bullshit," she mutters.

"Pizza doesn't mean anything," I tell Lulu.

"But butterflies for both of you does. Him not sleeping with you does. Him taking you to hidden gems does."

"Is there anything that doesn't?" I ask her.

Lulu shrugs. "I've known him his entire life. The

man doesn't move slow, and he's moving real damn slow. There's a reason for that."

"Because we're friends."

Lulu and Zoey chuckle in unison, but before they can say anything else, the woman walks out of the back, carrying a tray filled with cake slices. My mouth instantly waters at the heavenly scent.

"Here are the three finalists," she explains as she sets the tray on the table and starts to hand out the plates. "The white with the strawberry is the cassata. Then we have the chocolate overload. And last but not least, we have the Chantilly."

They're all beautiful in their own right. I've never been a dessert girlie, but a spread like this could have me changing my mind. How my brother would pass on this is beyond me.

"Why didn't Hunter come?" Lulu asks the same question I did.

"He helped pick these three. He couldn't decide and told me to surprise him."

"Good man," Lulu replies.

"He is," Zoey says with the biggest smile. "I don't know how I got so damn lucky."

"It's your boobs," Lulu tells her. "They're a magnet."

I giggle immediately.

"They're great, right?" Lulu asks me for confirmation.

"You both have great tits," I reply, earning myself a smile from them.

"Boobs are overrated. Don't get me started on the back pain that comes with them. And then there's pregnancy boobs." Lulu shakes her head. "The worst."

"Don't talk about pregnancy. Don't jinx me like that," Zoey tells her sister as she picks up her fork.

"You ladies are too damn cute," the bakery lady says before she tells us to take our time and enjoy the cakes.

"First, the cassata," Zoey says.

I'm thankful for a change in conversation. Cake is a safer topic. One I could go on about forever because it's way less complicated.

I am older than Zoey and Lulu, with no hope of being in Zoey's shoes anytime soon. I've been in a few relationships, but each one naturally fell apart with time —or the guy cheated on me when I already knew the relationship was over but didn't have the heart to end it before he strayed.

I always thought I'd be married by thirty, but the world has had other plans for me. Now, I'm not settling. I want everything and won't accept anything less. I have always pictured my wedding day, my stomach fluttering with anticipation of my happily ever after. I just never thought the first man to give me those butterflies would be someone I had no future with.

CHAPTER 3
MASON

"HEY." Nino slides onto a stool across from me, giving me one of his cocky smirks. "What's new?"

I don't even ask what he wants to drink. It's always the same. The man doesn't know how to be creative when it comes to his beverages. He likes one craft beer we've had on tap forever, and I don't think we'll get rid of it because it's popular with him and other people in the neighborhood.

"Nada," I tell him as I set down a full glass in front of him. "Same shit, different day."

He lifts the glass to his lips and pauses. "That's not what I heard."

I stare at him, searching his face for a clue. I don't want to get into anything with him, but my curiosity also won't let me walk away without hearing what he has to say. I lean forward, taking some of the pressure off my back. I've worked too long today, and my boots need to be replaced because I wore these out a month ago and my feet are getting tortured. "What did you hear?"

At that moment, Nino decides to take a sip. But not a short gulp…he slowly downs half the glass. Typical Nino. He likes to play games. Usually, I'm down for it, but since the topic has to do with me, I'm not exactly thrilled by his lack of speed.

Although I'm closest to Zoey out of all my cousins, it's because we work at the bar together every day and have for years. But Nino and I have always been thick as thieves since we're close in age.

But unlike me, Nino has gone the nontraditional route with life. While he says he's studying to be a tattoo artist and is going to be asking Tate for a job soon, he's somewhat of a hustler, which doesn't make Aunt Daphne and Uncle Leo very happy.

"I heard you have a date tonight, and you didn't tell me. I feel like you're hiding things from me."

"I didn't think I had to report everything."

"Uh, hello. Of course you do. Now, who's the chick?"

"You've met her."

He sets down his beer, leans back, and crosses his arms. "Recently?"

I nod.

"The lady at the bookstore?"

I snort and shake my head. "Nino, she's a little too old for me."

"Yeah, but she's hot as fuck. Am I right?"

"She is that," I tell him.

I almost fell over when Nino said he wanted to go to the bookstore. I didn't even know he read anything besides the dark sites he finds on the internet, learning how to better his hustle. And then he hit on the lady working there, trying to get her number. It was so odd to me and more than a little surprising.

"So, again, who's the chick?"

"Lizzy."

"Lizzy," he repeats, and I can tell by the vacant look in his eyes the name isn't clicking.

"Hunter's sister."

He sucks in a breath as his eyes widen. "You can't bang his sister, man. That's a big no-no. I do some fucked-up shit, but that's even beyond me."

"I'm not banging her."

The door to the bar opens, and my attention is drawn away from Nino. But to my shock, and maybe my horror, Amelia strides in with her head held high.

"Fuckin' great. Who's talking shit?" I ask him as my gaze drops to his face.

"I don't know what you mean," he mutters behind the rim of his beer glass.

"You and Amelia are here at the same time, and it's not a family dinner. Who opened their mouth?"

"About what?" He feigns innocence.

"My date."

"Aha," he barks and points a finger at me before setting down his beer.

"I'm here. I'm here," Amelia says, breezing through the bar like she comes here every day. "What'd I miss?"

"He just confessed about his date," Nino tells her as she sits down on the barstool next to him.

"Good. That's half the battle." Amelia gives me a smile as she shrugs off her coat. "What's the plan?"

"Plan?" I ask, looking between them. "There's no plan and no date."

"He just called it a date before you walked in."

"A woman like Lizzy doesn't just go out with a man. She dates," Amelia informs me. "Also, I want an espresso martini."

"Of course you do," I mutter before moving to make her drink. "You'd never drink something as plain as beer."

"Don't use the cheap stuff either. I want the creamy liqueur."

I sigh as I grab the top-shelf chocolate liqueur. "I wouldn't dream of using the cheap stuff on you, M."

The girl is high-class. She always has been, from a very young age. She and Nino are very much alike in that way. It's probably because they're only children with no siblings to share time, attention, and material things with. They were spoiled from the moment they were born and continue to be to this day.

"How's Uncle Vinnie?" I ask her.

"Pops is good. He's at the gym."

Where else would the man be? He retired years ago, but he continues to stay in shape and push himself just as hard as he did when he was training for the professional league.

"But I'm not here to talk about him. We're here to talk about you and Lizzy," she says as she takes the martini glass from my hands and studies it. "This looks perfect."

"We have nothing to talk about," I tell her. "And I have a bar to run."

Amelia glances around the dining area and then down the length of the bar, looking both ways. "Looks kind of dead to me. Don't make excuses."

"I love you both, but I'm old enough that I don't need dating advice from two people who are also single."

Amelia takes a sip of her martini and does a little dance in her seat, giving me a thumbs-up. "Maybe you don't need advice from him," she says with that same thumb toward Nino, "but you need advice from me because I'm a girl."

"You are?" I ask, doing my best to appear shocked by the news. "I didn't know. And that makes you a Lizzy expert?"

She nods. "You two have gone out a bunch, though, right?"

I nod, figuring I'll play along.

"Have you kissed?"

Man, they all are really nosy. Have my cousins

always been this way? Maybe I've been left out of the loop when it comes to this stuff, because I don't really have these discussions with Brax, Tate, Lulu, or Zoey.

"We're taking things slow."

"Does she know that?" Amelia asks.

"We're friends."

Amelia groans. "I know Lizzy likes you, and you like her. It's time to make the big move tonight, or else you're going to lose her forever."

"I don't know if you realize this, but she doesn't live in Chicago, M. I've never had a long-term girlfriend, let alone done long-distance dating."

Amelia stares at me over the rim of her martini, slurping the creamy liquid. She knows the sound annoys me, and that's why she does it for an excruciating length of time. When she sees my patience starting to fray, she pulls back, licks her lips, and gives me a devilish smile. "Well, that's a complication, but it doesn't make anything impossible. If you two like each other, distance won't matter."

"Are you making excuses because you're too scared to make a move?" Nino asks as he stares down at his phone. "I think you're chickenshit."

Am I chickenshit? Maybe a little. I'm so into her, and the thought of fucking it all up before we have a chance to get started makes my palms sweaty.

"I'm not chickenshit," I tell him because I've never been that man. At least, not before Lizzy.

I never cared if a woman shot me down. It's

happened more times than I'd like to admit, but it's never killed my ego or stopped me from trying again. But things are different with Lizzy. Not just because I really like her, but because her brother is marrying into the family. If things don't work out, we'll have to see each other for the rest of our lives. Awkward isn't even a strong enough word to describe that aftermath.

"Prove it," Nino says as he finally glances up from his phone with a wicked gleam in his eyes. He knows what he's doing.

"I have customers to take care of," I say, pushing myself away from the bar.

Amelia leans forward and looks at Marv. "Yeah, Marv looks like he needs a refill."

I give my cousin the middle finger.

"I could use another," Marv says, outpacing his normal beer an hour. I don't know how the man does it. I imagine he doesn't have just blood running through his veins. It has to be half booze, given the amount the man downs like it's water, and it doesn't affect him at all.

"What do you think, Marv?" Amelia asks him.

Marv's been around so long, he knows everything about our family, including the gossip.

"Should he make a move?" Amelia adds.

"He's too chickenshit," Marv mumbles, knowing damn well he's going to make me mad.

I cross my arms as I pin him with a glare.

He clears his throat as he says, "But I have faith in him. He'll do what he needs to do."

Amelia shakes her head as her lips flatten. "Marv, I thought you had a stiffer backbone than that," she says.

The door opens, and for a moment, I think I am saved from this conversation because I'll be too busy waiting on a new customer. My hopes are dashed as their face comes into focus.

"Hey," my dad says as he stalks toward the bar, untangling an extra fuzzy scarf from around his shoulders.

"Unc," Amelia and Nino say in unison as my father plops down onto a stool next to them.

My dad ran the bar for years with his siblings. He spent more hours here than I care to remember. He wasn't an absent father, but many nights were spent here instead of at home. Mom was with us at night since her bakery was busy in the morning and afternoon. Between the two of them, they had the entire day covered. We never spent time with babysitters. On rare occasions, my grandparents would watch us when Mom and Dad needed some alone time.

"Hey, kids. What are you two doing here?" he asks them.

"Bothering him," Amelia replies with a smirk.

"Making sure he doesn't screw up tonight," Nino adds.

Dad's eyebrows rise as his gaze moves to me. "What are you going to screw up?"

I sigh as I pinch the bridge of my nose and rub away the tension, or maybe it's annoyance. "I'm not going to screw anything up."

"He has a date with Lizzy," Amelia says, ratting me out.

"About damn time," Dad says.

I groan. "Not you too."

"Lizzy's a good girl, and if you're smart, you need to make a move before someone else does," he tells me.

"I know. I know. I've got this handled," I reply. "But it's complicated."

"I understand complicated love and relationships. But if it's meant to be, it's meant to be."

"And how do you know if it's meant to be, Unc?" Amelia asks, saving me from asking him myself.

He swivels his stool to face my cousins, leaning forward to glance down two spots at Amelia. "When you can't imagine your life without the other person, and the desire to be near them is more important than breathing."

"Oh. Is that all?" she says, teasing him.

"More or less," he mumbles.

"I hope that type of love finds me someday," she breathes.

"It will when you least expect it. I never thought I'd fall in love again, but then Tilly opened the shop next door, and the rest is history."

There's still sorrow in my father's eyes. I've seen old pictures of him, and his vibe is entirely different now.

Losing his first wife, Tate and Brax's mom, stole something from him that nothing in the world, including the love of my mother, could ever replace.

Is he happy? Yeah, my dad is a happy guy, but that doesn't mean there isn't a wound that can't ever be healed, no matter what joy he's found later in life. And my mom understands his pain since she lost her first husband. She doesn't question Dad's loyalty to her or his love because she knows the grief he's experienced and continues to deal with decades later.

Dad smiles as he turns back around, staring at his own reflection in the mirror behind the bar. "I'd say we were meant to be. If she hadn't opened the shop next door, I may have never met her. I'd hate to think of what life would be like without her in it."

"You were lucky Mom was right next door. Lizzy doesn't even live in this state," I tell him.

"Grab me a coffee, kiddo," Dad says. "I need something to take the chill out of my bones."

"Beer works better," Marv says, lifting his glass to my dad when they make eye contact.

"Good to see you, Marv," Dad replies with a kind smile. "You're looking well."

"I'm at my favorite spot. Nothing makes me happier," Marv tells him. "It's good for the soul."

When I look at the two men, I know I want to be like my father and not Marv. Dad is being nice, saying that Marv looks well. He lied through his teeth, though. Marv looks like shit. How could he not? He spends all day, every day here, drinking like there's no greater thing in life. I don't want to be a sad sack, sitting on a random barstool, nursing a beer alone, when I am in my sixties.

I grab my dad's coffee and set it in front of him, not bothering to grab the sugar and cream. The man has always taken it black, and no matter how many times I try it, it always makes my stomach sour.

"Son, distance doesn't matter when you love someone."

"I know, Dad, but we aren't there yet."

"I see the way you look at her. How you comforted her when her brother was in the hospital. You have feelings for Lizzy, even if you haven't figured out what they are yet."

"I'm working on it."

"Work harder and faster," he says, as if it's easy.

"Got it," I reply.

What else is there to say?

I can't get my hopes up. Lizzy has an entire life, and most of it isn't in Chicago. Sure, her brother is here and her niece, but I don't think that is enough to make her move to the big city. They've been here a while, and she hasn't done it. Would I be enough to make her finally decide to take the leap?

I guess I'll have to do everything in my power to give her a reason to uproot her life and start a new one with me.

CHAPTER 4
LIZZY

I GROAN as I stare at myself in the mirror, clutching my stomach. There's such a thing as too much cake. I tested the limits and lost. This is the last thing I need.

Mason didn't say tonight was a date, but for the first time, it feels like it could be. Something feels different this trip. The air is a bit heavier when Mason is around, and no matter how hard I try, I can't shake the pull I feel toward him.

"You look stunning," Zoey says, leaning in the bathroom doorway as she stares at my reflection.

"I wish I felt as good as you think I look."

She moves her hand to her stomach. "I'm feeling it too. Way too much sugar."

I relax a little at her words, figuring I'm not near a panic attack and that it is all the cake that is making my stomach a mess. "It was hard to resist."

"Yeah," she says as she pulls her phone from her back pocket. "Where are you two headed tonight?"

"I don't know." I lean forward, dabbing the inner corner of my eyes to smooth a rough patch of makeup. "Mason planned everything."

"You sure you two don't want to stay in and play a game with us?" she asks.

"No!" Hunter yells from the kitchen. "They want to go out."

I chuckle and shake my head. "My brother obviously doesn't feel the same."

"A man has needs!" he shouts back.

Zoey rolls her eyes. "Anyway, I hope you have fun. We won't wait up for you."

I turn around and face her. "Am I making a mistake?"

She straightens and tilts her head, looking at me like I've grown another limb. "Why do you ask that?"

I shrug, and the butterflies return, mixing with the aftermath of the wedding cake. "I really like him, and he really likes me. Are we just teasing ourselves? We live in two different states."

"Eh," she mumbles, waving me off. "Don't put that much thought into anything. Just have some fun tonight."

Don't put that much thought into anything? That's easier said than done. When I'm with him, nothing else matters. The world melts away, and I forget about the distance that's normally between us. But the moment he's away, all the doubts and reasons why I haven't let anything more happen come roaring back.

"Mason's here," Hunter calls from the living room.

My heart instantly picks up the pace, and my palms turn sweaty. "Wish me luck."

"Babe you've already got his full attention. I'm more worried about the cake in our bellies than you needing luck on this date."

The final word rings in my ears. *Date.* It's the elephant in the room. I consider Mason a good friend, someone I know I can lean on in times of need. But is he more? Are we both dancing around the word because we are equally scared to death of rejection and terrified of commitment?

It is laughable, really. A man like Mason Gallo doesn't fear rejection. The man is as smooth as fine wine, and I've seen the way the women at the bar, and just about everywhere else we go, fawn over him. Confidence oozes off him and draws women to him like moths to a flame.

"Thanks," I tell her, giving her a peck on the cheek before she steps aside, letting me leave the bathroom first.

"You've got this," she says from behind me as she follows me to the living room.

I snag my purse off the hook in the hallway, hooks I added because my brother didn't have anywhere to hang a damn thing. I always forget about all the little things men don't have to deal with, like purses. "I'm ready," I say as I gaze down at my outfit, making sure everything is in order.

When my head tips up and my eyes meet Mason's, I come to a stuttering stop. The man looks better than ever. How's that possible? I'm not entirely sure. Maybe my hormones are out of control, and my entire body is reacting to his closeness.

Mason has on black dress pants, a crisp white dress shirt with the sleeves rolled up, and a pair of black boots that are more on the dressy side than his usual. "Hey," he says, his voice smooth as butter.

"Hey," I say back, unable to think of some cute, pithy reply because my brain is on the fritz.

"Do you feel the crackle?" Zoey says behind me.

Normally, this type of situation wouldn't be so awkward, but with Zoey and Hunter staring at us, it's hella weird.

Mason's dark eyes never leave me, and he ignores his cousin and my brother as he holds out his hand. "Ready?"

"Yes," I breathe as my feet move forward until the tips of my fingers touch his.

He steadies me as I push my feet into my boots, wishing spring would stick. The constant change in weather from hot to cold has my head spinning.

I try to ignore the warmth of his hand as his fingers

curl around mine, but it's damn near impossible. The man is like a furnace, and my mind wanders, imagining snuggling up with him on a cold winter night.

"Don't wait up," he tells my brother and soon-to-be sister-in-law as I straighten. "We'll be out late."

I raise my eyebrows, but I don't say anything. It's nothing new. Mason's a night owl, and Zoey's no different. When you own a bar, nighttime is when you thrive. But for me, a woman with a corporate job, I am more of a morning person and drag ass as the hours pass.

"Have fun," Zoey calls out as Mason opens the door, ushering me into the hallway.

When we're alone, I finally feel like I can breathe because we don't have two extra sets of eyes on us. Being picked up by a man as an adult in front of my brother is somehow more awkward than what I experienced as a teenager with my parents as an audience.

"Where are we headed?" I ask as he stabs at the elevator button.

"It's a surprise, but I know you'll love it," he says, pulling me closer to his side.

—————

The restaurant is stunning. We don't have anything like this back home. The ceiling is glass with the stars of the clear night sky twinkling above us. The brick walls give the space a warm feel, along with the plants and books that line the walls.

"I don't think I've been to any place this fancy."

My hometown is simple. We have a few restaurants, many of which are only open for breakfast and lunch. They lack the ambiance and charm this place has in abundance.

Mason grabs the wine bottle, topping off my glass. "It's new. I've heard amazing things about the food, and I thought you'd love it."

"I do," I tell him as I take my glass, knowing I should slow down on the wine.

I haven't eaten much of anything all day besides the cake.

"I'm going to be drunk if the food doesn't come soon."

Mason smirks, and my stomach flips. "Would that be so bad?"

I smile, the alcohol making everything seem like a good idea, even the hangover that I'll inevitably have tomorrow. "I always drink too much with you."

He leans forward, staring me right in the eyes. "Why is that?"

I nearly swallow my own tongue over the heaviness of his gaze. "I don't know," I whisper, but I'm lying.

"I think you do," he replies. "Do I make you nervous?"

The breath in my lungs lodges in my throat as all the air in the restaurant seems to evaporate. "A little."

He slides his hand across the table, his fingertips

touching mine. "Don't be nervous, sweetheart. I won't hurt you."

"I know," I whisper, unable to tear my gaze away from his.

"Do you?"

"I do."

I know that about him. I know his family, and every interaction with Mason has always been great. The man makes my toes curl with a simple glance, and all his sweetness makes every fiber in my body come alive in his presence.

"I want to ask you something."

I search his face, trying to figure out what he's about to ask before he opens his mouth. I do my best to prepare myself for anything, but I've failed to think of the one thing he says next.

"Do you like me?" he asks.

I blink, staring at him. Is the man clueless? I may not fawn over him like other women, but I do turn into a fumbling idiot around him in a heartbeat. I always thought he clocked my weirdness, but maybe I hid it better than I thought.

"I do."

He smiles, and it's my turn to get a little bolder in my words and actions. The wine doesn't hurt when it comes to me living a little more dangerously.

"Do you like me?" I ask him back.

"I do."

I suck in a breath, wondering if we're playing with fire.

Mason is the one person in the city I count as a friend. In fact, he is more of a best friend and someone who doesn't have to hang out with me because we're related.

"What's stopping us?" he asks.

"About three hundred miles."

"Right. That." His voice is laced with humor, breaking the tenseness of the moment.

"And then there's the possibility we wouldn't work out. It would make holidays a bit…" My voice drifts off with my thoughts as I try to picture a future like that. One where Mason isn't in it as a friend, but a foe… someone who broke my heart.

"Shitty."

I nearly spit out the sip of wine that barely made it past my lips. "I was going for awkward, but shitty works too."

"Have you ever thought about moving?" he asks.

"A few times, especially since Hunter and Amira are here. I don't have any other family back home. The only thing keeping me there is my job, which I've spent over a decade carefully building."

"I'm sure you could find something comparable here in the city."

"Sure, but I'd be at the bottom instead of halfway up that impossible corporate ladder."

Mason wrinkles his nose. "I never wanted that life. How do you deal with the stress?"

I lift the wineglass. "This helps."

Mason's face softens as he stares at me across the table. "What are your life goals and dreams?"

I gaze at him as I lean back in my chair. The question throws me for a loop. It's a deeper topic than I'm used to when I hang out with him. We usually keep the conversation casual and light, but tonight, things are getting heavy in a hurry. "To be happy," I answer simply.

"And are you?"

"Not really," I admit, my voice softer than I expected. "I used to be, but I'm not really anymore."

"What's changed?" he pushes.

"Everything that matters to me is here."

"When we're old and have only a few heartbeats left, are you going to be happy you stayed for your job or sad for all the time you missed with the people most important to you?"

Damn. Why does he turn into such a sage at the most inopportune times? "I've thought about that a million times, Mason."

"Here we are," our waiter says, interrupting the topic before Mason can question me further. Hopefully the subject is dropped...at least for now.

"This looks amazing," I say as the man sets down my plate, and my mouth instantly waters from the aroma.

The presentation is over the top, exactly what I expect from a Chicago restaurant. Everything about the city is bigger and better than anything we have back home. Even the department store in the heart of downtown has multiple levels and is exhausting.

"Do you need anything else?" the waiter asks.

Mason looks at me, and I shake my head. "We're good. Thank you," he tells the waiter, and we're left alone again.

Before I have a chance to take my first bite, Mason asks, "Do you love your work?"

I stare at him as I place a piece of filet in my mouth. It instantly melts, and it gives me a moment to think about his question.

Do I love it? I've spent a decade climbing up to where I am now. I'd thought by the time I got to this level, I'd be filled with joy, but the complete opposite is true. The pressure is more. The stress is greater. Nothing seems to be as sweet as it was when I first started in the business.

"Do you love yours?"

"I do. Every day is different. Life at the bar is far from boring."

"Is it stressful?" I ask.

"Nah. It's always a good time."

I'm more than a little envious of the look in his eyes when he talks about the Hook & Hustle. I don't remember the last time I thought my job was a good time.

"I refuse to do anything that doesn't bring me joy. Life's too short to be miserable, Lizzy."

I know better than anyone how quickly our time on earth can end. My parents were young when they passed, compared to most of the world's population.

"Change isn't easy for me."

"I think that's true for most people, but sometimes it's worth the hassle for whatever comes after."

CHAPTER 5
MASON

IT'S WELL after one in the morning when we near the block where my cousin lives. "You want a donut? The place around the corner has *the* best you'll ever have in your life."

"I don't know," Lizzy says, placing her hand on her stomach. "Do you know how much cake I ate today?" She keeps pace at my side, our hands brushing every few steps.

"Is there such a thing as too much cake?"

In my family, there's no such thing as too much anything. We overindulge in all things, and I don't hate it.

"If I'm not careful, I won't be able to fit in my clothes anymore because of your family."

I turn my head, wanting to make eye contact with her when I say, "Sweetheart, you're already far too skinny."

"You sound like your grandmother."

"She's smart."

"She is, but not when it comes to the amount of food she puts on my plate."

"You'd look good with a little more meat on your bones."

"Now you sound like your mother."

"Real men don't want skin and bones," I tell her.

She stops walking. "I'm not too big?"

I turn and stalk toward her. When I get close, I raise my hand, taking her chin between my thumb and index finger. When she tips her head up, her eyes meet mine. "You're perfect."

Her cheeks turn a deeper shade of pink, already rosy from the cold. "I…"

"Whoever told you that you were too big is an asshole. I want my woman soft. I want something to hold. Skin and bones doesn't do it for me, and if a man is worth his weight in salt, that wouldn't do it for him either."

She squeezes her eyes shut and swallows. "I could lose a few pounds."

I step closer, keeping my hand at her chin. "Look at me, Lizzy."

Her shoulders slump before she opens her eyes.

There's pain in those eyes. Something that's buried deep. Probably some shit planted by an ex-boyfriend who had a tiny dick and had to compensate for it by tearing her down.

"You. Are. Perfect."

She reaches out, pressing her hand to my abdomen. "You're all hard muscle underneath here. You can eat a donut and not think a thing about it. You're not judged based on what you look like, but I am."

"Does their opinion matter—or mine?" I ask, pausing for a second, but not giving her a chance to answer. "Because everything I see is something I want."

Her eyes widen as she swallows roughly.

"If you were mine, I'd touch, lick, and kiss every single inch of your body and be the happiest man on the planet while doing it. You only live once. Eat the donut. Be fucking happy. If a man doesn't love you for what's in your heart and worship your body while doing it, he ain't shit, sweetheart."

She sways a little, and I wrap an arm around her, pulling her close and giving her body support. Our mouths are nearly touching. The warmth of her rapid breath skids across my cold skin.

"I want to kiss you," I tell her. We've never crossed this bridge. We've come close more than once, but I've never let myself do it. I didn't want to mess up the good thing we have going, but time is slipping away. Days have turned into weeks, which have turned into months. It is time for me to shit or get off the pot.

"Where?" she asks and smirks.

"First, here," I say, brushing my lips against her cheek, and she sucks in a breath, nearly melting in my arms. "And here." I slide my lips to her ear, breathing heavy and moaning as I suck her earlobe. But I don't get stuck there, wanting to taste her mouth more than I want to breathe. "And here." My words come out soft as I meet her eyes, searching them for anything that tells me to stop. But I don't see that in her gaze. There's hunger there. The same burning she probably sees in my eyes too.

My mouth touches hers softly, testing the waters, but I know I have her when she curls her fingers around my shirt and fists the material. Her chest presses against mine as she tips her head back, tilting her head to the side.

I groan as I taste her lips, the wine from dinner lingering on her skin. I trail my fingers from her chin to her cheek, cradling her face in my hand. I move my other hand, holding the middle of her back, and press her harder against me. The heat between us blocks out the bitter cold that's plagued the city for months.

My body feels like it's on fire, the need for her burning me up from the inside. I've never felt this way before with anyone. Maybe it's because we didn't get physical immediately. Or maybe it's the want that's been growing in me for months without taking any steps to feed the need that is practically at a fever pitch.

"Mason," she moans against my lips as I slip my tongue inside her mouth and lose myself in her.

I could do this forever and be happy. If I could

freeze a moment in time and stay there until my dying breath, this would be it.

A siren blares through the narrow street, causing Lizzy to jump. The magical moment is instantly ruined. I stare at her and she stares at me, our breaths ragged and labored.

"Wow… That was…" she says, stopping to suck in a breath.

"Yeah," I whisper to her, forcing the words out as I gather my thoughts. Our bodies are still connected everywhere else as we gaze into each other's eyes.

She shivers as a gust of wind nearly forces her away from me, but she only tightens her grip on my shirt. "Everything's so loud here."

Fucking cops. If I didn't know better, I'd say he did that shit on purpose to ruin our moment. He could've waited until he cleared the block to turn on his sirens. We hadn't seen a car on the street for a block. The city's always alive, but this part of town was quieter at this hour.

"I'd better get you home," I tell her.

If she weren't Hunter's sister, I'd invite her over and finish what we started. But I promised myself I'd take things slow with her. I'd do everything in my power not to have us end in a way that would make the rest of our lives awkward.

"Oh. Okay," she says, dropping her hands away from my sides.

I can see the disappointment in her eyes at my suggestion, and I hate myself for putting it there.

"It's not that I don't want to continue, but it's late, and I want to do things right with you and by you."

"Do things right?" She smiles, drawing my attention to her lips again.

I tip my head, dropping my forehead to hers. "I want you so bad, Lizzy. Worse than I've ever wanted anyone before, but I don't want to screw anything up. We have a good thing going here, and I want to make sure you and I will both survive if we go any deeper."

"I understand," she whispers and sighs. "I think you could easily break my heart."

I have nothing to say to that. While what she is saying is true, my bigger fear is that she could shatter mine and I'd never recover.

"Come on," I say, pulling her to my side to finish the last stretch to the apartment building.

We walk in silence, the heaviness of what just happened hanging between us. Have we already gone past the point of no return? Are things already awkward with no chance of recovery? Did I mess things up more by slowing things down and not finishing what we started on the street just a few minutes ago? God, I fucking hope not.

"Shit," Lizzy snaps and then gasps.

I turn my head, seeing her wide eyes. I follow her line of sight and realize what has drained her face of color.

"Is that your car?" I ask her, shaking my head.

"It was," she whispers, her voice wobbling like she's ready to burst into tears.

You don't grow up with a sister and not pick up on signs that the waterworks are about to start. And for damn good reason, too.

Her car is smashed in, the entire driver's side demolished. She's parked on the street near the building since indoor parking is limited and only for residents.

"Shit," I snap, unable to believe my eyes. "Damn. That's bad."

"Fuck," she says again, and there's just something about her saying dirty words that does crazy things to me. "What am I going to do now? I'm supposed to drive home tomorrow."

"I got you, sweetheart."

She glances around, ignoring my words. "Who did this? Did they just leave?"

"Happens all the time."

"That's so rude and illegal," she says, and it's so damn cute. I can tell she lives her life in a certain way and is shocked anytime someone else doesn't.

"People do far worse shit than that."

"What do I do, Mason?" She looks at me, needing some guidance. She's probably in shock, and it's my time to shine.

"We'll call Oliver. He'll tow the car and get it off the

street. We can figure the rest out later. I'll take you home tomorrow. Zoey can cover my shifts."

Lizzy turns to me, her eyes swimming with tears. "You'd do that?"

"What? Drive you home?"

"Yeah," she whispers, clinging on to me like I'm her lifeline.

"Sweetheart, there's no place I'd rather be. If you need a ride, I'll give it to you. Whatever you need, I'll be the one to make it happen."

She drops her head to my chest, her fingers curled around the sides of my jacket. "I hate that you have to go out of your way. It's not a quick trip."

"Six hours stuck in a car with you doesn't sound like a bad time."

"You've clearly never driven through Indiana," she mutters into the material of my jacket. "It's a whole lot of nothing."

"But you'll be there, and that's all that matters. And I'll finally be able to see what makes your small town so special."

"It's not," she says, peering up at me as a tear slides down her cheek.

I reach up, wiping it away. I wish I could take away her pain and stress in this moment, but all I can do is make the blow a little less painful. "If you're there, it is."

"You're smooth, Mason. Real smooth."

I rub my nose against hers, and it's nearly frozen.

"Come on. Let's get you inside, and Oliver and I will handle the rest."

"Okay," she whispers, and there's a moment when I think about kissing her again, but I don't.

Now isn't the time.

Her emotions are too all over the place about what happened to her car.

There will be time for another.

Hopefully, we have an eternity.

Thirty minutes later, Oliver pulls up outside Hunter and Zoey's place. As soon as he's out of his truck, he shakes his head and whistles. "Someone did a number on this thing."

"Think it's fixable?" I ask him, trying to control my body from shaking due to the cold.

"Not a damn chance, but I'll tow it to the shop so her insurance can look it over."

"Sorry about this," I tell him as I tuck my hands into my pockets to try to find warmth.

"No problem. I was on call tonight. No skin off my neck. Want a ride home?"

"Please," I tell him, my voice shaking as I shiver.

"Get in the truck and warm up while I hook this thing up."

"You think you can tow it?"

"I've towed worse."

"What's worse? There's not much left of this one."

He chuckles. "I've seen some shit."

"I'm sure."

"Get in," he says, ticking his head toward the cab while he stalks toward the back of his tow.

"I'll wait out here with you."

I'm not getting in to warm up while he stands out here in the cold. No way. I'm not that man. I wasn't raised that way. Maybe if Oliver were a stranger, I would, but he's family and doing me a solid.

"She need a rental?" he asks, making a ton of noise moving some levers.

"No. I'm going to drive her home tomorrow."

"Take my car."

I know it probably seems weird to some people that I don't have my own car, but I rarely leave the city. Every place I need to go can be accessed via the El or a taxi if I can't walk. It's one of the things I love about Chicago. Plus, the cost of a parking spot in my building is ridiculous, and that doesn't include insurance and a car payment on top of it. I never felt the need for a car, just for it to sit in the underground garage and rot.

"You sure?" I ask him.

"One hundred percent. It's a fun ride too."

"I have a lead foot."

"Then it'll be extra fun," he says with a chuckle.

He has a muscle SUV. He took me for a ride in it when he got it, and I practically had a heart attack when he floored it. The thing damn near flew across the road, and I swear the front end even got some air.

"Thanks, Oli."

"What else is family for?" he says.

And that is the thing about being here. I have a big family, and I'll never leave them. If Lizzy won't move here, there is no future for us because I know I'll never leave the life I have here.

But that only means it is officially time I put more pressure on her and make her realize everything she wants and needs is here in Chicago and with me.

CHAPTER 6
LIZZY

SIX HOURS PASSED IN A BLUR. When I'm alone and listening to an audiobook, it goes by quick, but nowhere near the speed it did with Mason in the car with me. The conversation never stopped. There were no awkward pauses where we struggled to think of things to say to each other. It was refreshing and shocking all at the same time.

"So, this is it, huh?" he asks as we pull into the center of town, and he stops at the traffic light at the main intersection.

It's quaint and beautiful. No building is over three stories tall, and we have a gazebo in the town center, surrounded by a little park. Small businesses line Main Street, many of them started generations prior.

"This is it. This is Star Falls."

"It's cute. Reminds me of something I'd see in a movie."

I glance around, soaking in the scenery I've taken for granted my entire life because it's the only place I've ever lived. The unique beauty became part of the background noise of my everyday life. "It's cute but also extremely boring compared to Chicago."

"I can see why you love it so much."

"I used to love it. I thought it was the best place ever, but lately…"

"It doesn't feel like home anymore?" he asks, and I swear there's a hint of hopefulness in his voice.

"It's lost its sparkle, but mostly because my brother isn't here anymore."

"You know where he is?" he asks, teasing me.

"Where?" I ask, playing his game.

"Where I am." He gives me a smile that stops my heart for a second.

The man is handsome as the devil—tempting as him too. I'll never forget the first time I saw him at the bar. I nearly swallowed my own tongue. Never in a million years would I have thought I'd be here with him now. And even more, I never would've guessed he'd be doing his best to try to lure me away from here.

"I know," I say with a sigh, wishing it were so easy to move to another state. I do have a life here. A boring one, but it's still a life.

"Are you hungry? Is there any place good in town?"

"I'm starving. What do you want to eat?"

"Italian," he answers, but from the way he's looking at me, I feel like he'd rather have me.

Of course an Italian man is going to want to eat Italian. "Benito's is by the next light. They are the best in town."

"Is it Chicago good, though?"

"You're such a food snob," I tease him, swatting his arm playfully.

"It's hard not to be."

"You'll love Benito's. You're a lot like him and his family."

"Is he ridiculously handsome?" Mason asks, clearly needing his ego stroked.

"Not as handsome as you," I tell him. I know how to play the game.

He lifts his chin a little higher with the compliment.

"Park here." I point to an open street spot near the restaurant.

Mason parallel parks like a pro. I still struggle with getting the angle right, and it takes me multiple tries before my car is perfect. When I have to do it in Chicago, it's always stressful because people are less patient than here.

Mason hasn't even made it to the sidewalk before I'm stopped by Marilyn, an old friend of my parents. "Sweetie, you're looking well."

"Thanks, Mar. You too. How have you been?"

Marilyn is stunning. For a woman in her sixties, she has very few wrinkles. I'd never guess her age if I didn't know her. Her hair is long and mostly gray, but there are still hints of black scattered throughout.

"Getting old isn't for the faint of heart," she says, tiny lines deepening around the corners of her eyes. "But it's still a blessing. I try to remember that when I feel down, honey."

I know what she's saying. My parents weren't lucky enough to grow old. They didn't have the gift of time like most people do, including Marilyn.

I pat her hand that's resting on my arm. "I know, Mar."

Her gaze swings to who I can only assume is Mason because her eyes widen. "Oh. Who do we have here?"

"I'm Mason. Lizzy's friend," he says, offering his hand to Marilyn. When she slides her hand into his, he lifts her fingers to his mouth and places a kiss against her skin.

Oh. He's a smooth one.

Marilyn's face immediately turns a bright shade of pink. "Lizzy's friend."

"He's Hunter's fiancée's cousin," I add, "and my friend."

"You're a handsome bugger, aren't you?" Marilyn asks, not pulling her hand out of his grasp. "Lizzy's lucky to have you as a friend."

"I'm the lucky one, ma'am," he replies, his arm at his side brushing against mine.

"Marilyn, is this your grandson?" Cathy, another old friend of my mother's, stops and asks.

"No, Cathy. This is Lizzy's friend." Marilyn finally lets her hand slide out of Mason's.

I do my best to stop myself from rolling my eyes. I can't imagine what Mason's thinking. We haven't made it a foot and have already been stopped by two people.

"Oh," Cathy says, sounding very much like Marilyn as she places her hand across her chest. "Well... I..."

"I know." Marilyn shoulder bumps Cathy. "He's a lot to take in."

Mason chuckles, and I'm pretty sure he's loving the attention. The man gobbles it up, but somehow, he isn't cocky with me—at least, not all the time.

"I hate to cut this short, ladies, but I need to get some food in Lizzy. She hasn't eaten all day," Mason tells them.

"Of course. Don't be a stranger," Marilyn says, her eyes moving between Mason and me. "Come on, Cathy. We have a lot to talk about."

The "a lot to talk" about is no doubt Mason and me. I also knew that within an hour, a majority of the town would know about Mason being here because the older ladies spread gossip faster than any social media app ever could.

I take Mason's hand, pulling him toward the door and off the street before we're stopped by someone else. His fingers intertwine with mine, and my stomach flutters at the contact and the intimate gesture. When he's around me, he has a sweetness to him that makes him even more irresistible.

The smell inside Benito's makes my stomach growl, and my mouth waters.

"It passes the smell test," Mason says as we move toward the hostess stand.

Rita's there, as always, her face covered in a smile. Rita's just like Cathy and Marilyn. She's a gossip, and since she works at the best restaurant in town, she knows everything.

"Lizzy," she says, her eyes on Mason and not me. "Table for two?"

I'm usually in here alone and sit at the bar. I don't love eating alone, but I also don't like having to cook for myself every night. The bar is a great option for me since it's usually filled with locals I've known my entire life, so it's never lonely or quiet.

"Please," I tell her.

"Right this way," she says, grabbing two menus even though I have the damn thing memorized.

Mason's hand doesn't leave mine as we weave our way through the crowded dining room. I don't need to look around to know all eyes are on me or, I should say, us.

This is the reason small-town living has been getting on my nerves lately. When I was younger, I never minded the way people watched every move I made, but the older I get, the more annoyed I find myself becoming.

Thankfully, Rita doesn't stick around as she tucks us into a booth near the back of the restaurant. It gives us a moderate amount of privacy.

"Was it me, or was everyone watching us?" he asks

as he makes himself comfortable and picks up the menu.

"It wasn't you."

"It's sweet."

"It's not," I argue as I glance up from the menu.

"Everyone loves you."

"You'd think that, but they're only excited to have something new to talk about. I'm not usually the topic of town gossip."

Mason chuckles and shakes his head. "Don't think this doesn't happen at my bar too. The regulars have a lot to say about everyone and everything."

"I haven't noticed that, but I feel anonymous when I'm there."

"They're good at hiding it," he tells me, his gaze moving to the menu in his hands. "Now, what's the best thing on the menu?"

"If you want something filling and rich, go with the lasagna. If you want something light, the lemon chicken is divine."

"Which one are you having?"

"The chicken." The last thing I want is to feel like a beached whale all night. I love the lasagna, but all the gluten makes me bloated.

"I'll have whatever you're having."

"You sure? You look more like a lasagna guy."

He raises an eyebrow as his gaze meets mine. "I look like a lasagna guy?"

"You don't get those—" my eyes dip to his muscular biceps "—from watching how much you eat."

"I eat a lot of protein, but I've never been one to care much about calories or carbs."

"Lucky," I mutter. Everything that goes into my mouth instantly settles in my gut, ass, and thighs.

"Who hurt you, sweetheart?"

My belly flutters at his words. "What?"

"Who made you think like that?"

"Like what?" I ask, setting the menu down in front of me.

Before he has a chance to answer, Benito's standing next to our table with a big smile. "Bella, we've missed you," he says, bending over to kiss each of my cheeks. "Rita told me you brought a guest, and I had to come out and say hello and meet your new friend."

I smile up at Benito. I've known him and his family my entire life. "This is Mason. He lives in Chicago."

Benito's face lights up before he turns toward Mason and extends a hand to him. "Welcome to my restaurant. I'm Benito, and any friend of Lizzy's is a friend of mine."

Mason shakes Benito's hand, staring at him in a way that makes me think that Mason's leery of Benito's kindness. "Thank you. I've heard only good things."

"Let me offer a treat for your table. I have a pot of artichokes in the back that I've been making all day. I'd love to send two out for you two to enjoy."

"That would be amazing," Mason says, his eyes lighting up.

"I don't think I've ever had artichoke outside of a jar," I say.

Benito clutches his chest, rocking back like I've wounded him. "That's a crime. You must try mine. It's an old family recipe."

"Whatever you want, Benny," I tell him. "If you make it, I'll eat it. You've never given me anything even remotely bad."

"Artichokes are the bomb," Mason says. "We're also each going to have the lemon chicken."

"Perfecto," Benito replies. "I'll send out a bottle of white wine that'll pair perfectly with both."

"You're too kind," Mason says to Benito.

It's like watching kindred spirits meeting for the first time.

"It's my pleasure. I need to get back to the kitchen, but I'll come check on you later. I'll be interested to see what you say about the artichokes, Lizzy."

"I'm sure I'll love them," I tell Benito.

He gives a quick bow before he disappears.

"He seems nice," Mason says, taking my menu and placing it with his on the edge of the table.

"He is, and so is his entire family."

"Now." Mason leans forward, clasping his hands on the table in front of him. "I want to know who hurt you, sweetheart?"

"What do you mean?"

"When I first met you, I thought you were this confident woman, but I've heard you say more than one thing about your body and image. Who put that shit in your mind? Who made you feel like it mattered?"

I shrug, trying to shut out the memories of my ex and his words that stung each time he made a comment about my body. "It's not a big deal."

Mason reaches out, taking my hand in his. "It is a big deal, Lizzy. No one should make you feel that way. Your body is absolute perfection."

I laugh nervously, but the look in his eyes says he's serious. "I have a few pounds to lose."

"Where?" he asks, staring at me. "I don't like a skinny woman. I don't want to hold skin and bones. I want lush. I want soft. Everything about your body and mind is perfect, except your opinion of yourself."

I never thought about my weight until Benjamin. He had a lot of opinions and would often order for me when we went out to eat because he said I wasn't healthy enough and he was doing me a favor.

"I don't think badly about myself. I'm just stating a fact," I tell him, squirming in my seat under the weight of his gaze.

"You do think badly about yourself. Who made you feel that way?"

"No one."

His lips set in a firm line. "Who?"

I sigh, my shoulders sagging forward. "You're like a

magazine model, Mason. You're covered in muscles. You're absolutely perfect."

"I'm not, but what does that have to do with how you feel about yourself?"

I open my mouth to reply, but I don't know how to answer at first.

"What would it take for you to believe me and not the asshole who made you feel less than?"

A million filthy things flash through my mind. "You could have anyone," I whisper.

"I want you."

I suck in a breath, but even though I want to believe him, I find it hard to. I clear my throat, suddenly warm.

"Here we go," Amanda, our waitress, says, setting down a plate with two artichokes and a bottle of wine. "It's good to see you again, Lizzy." She reaches for my wineglass, but I can see her stolen glances at Mason. He's a lot to look at, especially since he's new and drop-dead gorgeous.

"You too, Amanda. This is my friend Mason."

Her eyes finally land on him and stay there for a minute. "It's nice to meet you." Her face flushes as she speaks to him, soaking in his ruggedly handsome face.

"Nice to meet you too," he says, and when she hands him his glass of wine, he hands it to me, waiting for the next glass for himself.

"If you need anything else, please let me know," she says to him and not me. I don't blame her. She sees my face all the time, but a man as good-looking and new as he is doesn't roll into town very often.

"Thank you," he tells her, and she quickly disappears.

I stare at the artichoke, wondering how the hell I'm supposed to eat something like that. It looks like a cooked cactus, and nothing about it resembles the ones I buy in the jar.

"You peel off a leaf and use your teeth to scrape everything off," Mason explains as he plucks off a single piece.

I stare at him as he places it between his lips, slowly pulling it out. It's kind of erotic and completely messy, but I could seriously watch him eat an artichoke every single day of my life and be a happy woman.

I mimic his movements and am surprised by how easy the leaf comes off. I stare at it for a beat, looking at the breadcrumbs and whatever else is on it before placing it in my mouth. There's an explosion of flavors, and I moan a little before pulling out the leaf, scraping it against my teeth like he did. It's odd but surprising how delicious it is.

"My grandma used to make these all the time," he tells me, reaching for more.

"You're lucky she's such a good cook."

"She's not." He laughs and shakes his head. "She's an okay cook, but she has a few dishes she does well, and artichokes are one of them."

"I thought she was the main cook in the family."

"No. Family dinner is a group effort. My grandfather definitely didn't marry her for her cooking."

"They're totally adorable together," I tell him, wondering what it would be like to be with someone so long.

"They're something. My grandmother has put up with a lot of shit from Pops. He's a wild one."

"Still?" I ask.

"Still." He nods in confirmation. "He may not be completely in the game anymore, but he's not all the way out either."

"The game?" I ask in confusion. "Does he play baseball?"

My question earns me a chuckle from Mason. "No, sweetheart. He's been involved in things that weren't always on the up-and-up."

"The up-and-up?"

"Have you ever watched any mobster movies?"

I shake my head as my mind reels. "I'm more of a rom-com girlie."

"We'll need to change that."

I lean forward and whisper, "Are you saying your grandpa is in the mob?"

"I don't think he was ever fully in, but he also wasn't out."

"You're confusing me, Mason." I chuckle too, because surely he has to be pulling my leg. "That sweet man could never…"

"He could and he has. Ask anyone in the family. They know."

I lean back, my mouth gaping open in complete and utter shock. The man is so damn sweet. He's truly a Casanova and could charm the pants off anyone, men included. "I can't believe it," I mutter.

"You'll learn," he says.

"You're not involved, are you?" I need to know the answer before I let my heart start falling even deeper for the man sitting across from me.

"Never," he replies quickly.

"Good. Good."

"Now, eat up. Cold stuffed artichokes aren't good," he tells me, pushing the plate in my direction. "I need my girl to have a full belly after such a long day on the road."

I like being called his girl. I shouldn't. Neither of us is built for long-distance, but I can't seem to let myself wonder what it would be like to be loved by a man like him.

CHAPTER 7
MASON

STAR FALLS IS something straight out of an old television sitcom. Small shops line the main street that is, funnily enough, called Main Street. People are everywhere, walking and talking to each other without a care in the world or a need to be somewhere in a hurry.

"What's this?" I ask, pointing to the white building that has a line out onto the sidewalk.

"The ice cream shop."

I'm so full. I couldn't possibly add another thing to my stomach. She was right about Benito's. The food was better than I would've thought a small town like this could ever have.

"Want some?" she asks as my footsteps slow.

I place my hand on my stomach and debate whether I want to put myself into a food coma for the rest of the night. Then throw in the fact that it's still cold outside, and it's a solid no from me. "No," I say, but my voice lacks conviction.

Lizzy bumps me with her shoulder and leans into my space. "Are you sure? It's really good."

"Next time."

She trips, and I reach out to catch her before she can face-plant on the sidewalk in front of everyone. "Are you okay?" I glance around, wondering what the hell made her foot catch.

"You're going to come back?" she asks as she straightens, but she doesn't immediately move away from my grip.

"Why not? It's cute as hell here," I tell her, soaking in all the small-town vibes before I head back to Chicago tomorrow.

While the town is busy, it has a quietness to it that has my mind more at peace than it usually is back home. It's like all the background noise has been turned off.

"It's cute?" She wrinkles her nose as she glances around like she sees something different than I do.

As we cross a bridge, it's my turn to nearly trip over thin air. "What the..." I move to the metal railing and lean over. "This is stunning."

"It's the falls," she says, as if it's not a big deal. "Hence, Star Falls."

"I've never seen a waterfall in person," I whisper, unable to stop staring at the rushing water.

There's a soothing quality to the sound of the water rushing downstream and falling over the edge at break-neck speed. I could stand here all day and watch the water go by, letting go of everything else my mind is unable to block out.

"We can go down there." She points to a wooden platform near the water's edge about thirty feet below us.

"Really?" I hadn't even noticed a few people down there already because I was so transfixed by the water.

"Come on," she says, pulling my sleeve.

We cross back in front of the ice cream shop, and we come to a staircase almost hidden on the other side. We'd walked right by it, and I never noticed it. If I hadn't been here with her, I would've missed the chance to get close to the waterfall. The first one I've ever seen in person in my entire life.

The water gets louder with each step we take down toward the main platform. I clasp her hand in mine, wanting to make sure she doesn't tumble down the creaky wooden stairs. The area is thick with trees, giving it a fairy-tale vibe. I glance across the river, finding the other side lined with restaurants that over-look the falls.

"I want to eat there next time," I tell her, pointing toward the two-story glass-enclosed restaurant with my free hand.

"If you come back, I'll make reservations."

"I'll be back," I tell her as we step down onto the main section of the platform that lines a fifty-foot walkway on the edge of the river. "I'll need to see this again."

She turns and looks at me, a carefree and beautiful smile on her face. "Yeah?"

"And then there's you. I need to see you again too." I squeeze her fingers.

Her smile widens as she tilts her head, not breaking our physical contact. "You see me all the time in Chicago."

I tug her hand, pulling her into my arms. The place is magic, and I can't help but get swept away by everything around us. Jesus, my thoughts are a jumbled mess, and somehow, I sound more like my sister than myself. "I don't see you nearly enough."

Her breath hitches as she gazes into my eyes. "What's gotten into you?" she whispers, our lips almost touching.

"You," I whisper back before tipping my head, taking her lips in a hard, fast kiss. I can't help myself. I don't care who sees us or how small this community is. Let the gossips yell that they saw us kissing from the mountaintops. I want the world to know that I want this woman more than I want the air I breathe.

It's never been so easy to be around someone. She feels like home, like we were always meant to be together. Our bodies fit perfectly together. There are no awkward movements in the way our bodies mold to each other.

The world around us melts away. The murmurs of the crowd above and on the riverside disappear as if we're in a fever dream and no one else exists in the world except us.

I tangle my fingers in her hair as I cradle the back of her neck, loving the warmth of her skin against my cool hands. She gasps at the contact, but the sound disappears as I kiss her deeper, sliding my tongue between her open lips.

She tastes like wine again. This is the second time we've kissed, and both times she's tasted of something I've spent my entire life drinking in my Italian family.

"I want you," I murmur against her lips, unable to keep those words to myself any longer. The need to be with her in every physical way possible is becoming overwhelming.

"I want you too," she pants as she breaks the kiss, placing her hand on my chest.

Our eyes are locked. Her green to my brown. Our breaths are rushed, as if we've been underwater without air for longer than humanly possible.

She shoves me away, and it's as if someone poured a bucket of cold water over my head. "What the…"

"Not here," she says, glancing around.

I follow her gaze, and more than a few people are watching us intently.

"I wasn't planning on bending you over the railing."

Her face turns an even brighter shade of pink. "Jesus, Mason. That's a visual."

"A good one, though, amirite?" I say, moving us toward the very spot she's picturing herself bent over.

Our hips touch as we rest our body weight against the railing, staring across the water. My breathing still hasn't returned to normal, nor has my heart rate.

I slide my arm over, making every inch of our sides touch that can. "So, now what?"

She glances over for the briefest of moments. "I don't know. This is complicated."

"We can just do more of that." I tick my head toward where we were standing when we kissed. "I have all the time in the world until you want more."

"I want more," she says to the water. "My body does, but my heart is saying to slow down."

I can't blame her, but I want to argue and say we've known each other for months and months. Long enough that my cousin and her brother have dated and gotten engaged. Soon, they'll be married, and we haven't moved beyond first base.

I'm a patient man.

I can be a patient man.

I'll continue to be a patient man.

Lizzy's worth it. I don't want to do anything that'll jeopardize what we've been building for nearly a year. I don't want her to move faster than she wants and ruin everything before we really have a chance to get started.

"We'll wait for your heart to catch up with the rest of you," I promise her.

Something more is brewing under the surface. Maybe it's the man who made her feel like shit about her body. Someone messed with her mind about beauty, love, and relationships. I'll do whatever it takes to change the way she thinks about herself.

"Thanks," she says, leaning farther into me and resting her head on my shoulder. "You're a good man, Mason."

"I haven't always been," I confess, knowing my not-so-illustrious past and the sins I've committed.

I wasn't always the best person to date. I haven't thought too much about it, but my sister swears it's because of our father's history.

"Eh, we all have pasts. None of that matters."

I stare down at her as I wrap an arm around her back. "You're a remarkable woman, Lizzy."

She peers up, her green eyes shimmering. "I know."

I lean forward, brushing my lips against her forehead. If I could freeze a moment in time, this would be it. "Thank you for this."

"For what?" Her green eyes search mine.

"For bringing me here."

"You can thank the hit-and-run driver for that."

"You're right. If they ever catch him, I'll have to send a thank-you card."

She elbows me in the stomach. "You'd better send him a knuckle sandwich."

I grunt at the impact, doubling over to make her think her blow hurt me, when it didn't. I've taken harder jabs from my little cousins.

"Oh my God. I'm so sorry," she says with wide eyes.

I chuckle because she's so panicked. "I'm fine. You didn't hurt me, sweetheart."

"Jerk."

I wink at her. "Just needed to remind you I'm not as good all the time as you think I am."

Her eyes narrow, which is better than the fear I saw a moment ago. "I know you're a devil, but I think I like the wickedness in you."

"You've always liked bad boys, haven't you?"

"I've never dated one. Maybe that's been the problem."

"No. Wrong. We're a world of trouble, but eventually, we grow up."

"Are you grown now?" she asks with hopefulness in her eyes.

"I'm on my way there. But I also know I'm not the same shithead I was a few years ago."

"So, it's the right time?"

"Right time for what?" I ask, wanting her to say the words.

"For more."

Not exactly the answer I was hoping for, but it isn't one I am disappointed in either. "You want to get out of here?"

She swallows, indecision etched on her face.

"Not to do that." I won't lie. My hopes are a little dashed, but not completely. I don't want her to go faster than she wants, but I also want some contact…any contact with her. "Maybe we can watch some television and kiss a little like we're kids again."

She turns, placing her back against the railing, and stares up at me with narrowed green eyes. "How old were you when you had your first kiss?"

"The typical age."

Her hand moves to my chest as she tilts her head. "What's the typical age?"

I laugh. "How old were you?"

"Eighteen," she says.

I jerk my head back and stare at her in disbelief. "Eighteen?"

She nods.

"Tongue or no tongue?"

"No tongue."

"Seriously?" I ask, not believing her.

"Seriously." She nods. "Why? How old were you?"

"Tongue or no tongue?"

"Both," she replies.

"No tongue ten, and tongue twelve."

Her mouth falls open as she stares at me. "You think that's typical?"

"Well, yeah. But based on your face, I'd say you don't feel the same. But I also don't think eighteen is typical for no tongue. How old were you when you had your first French kiss?" I ask.

"My first kiss was with you."

"Liar," I say, shaking my head. "You've been yanking my leg the entire time."

She shrugs. "Let's go." She takes my hand, pulling me toward the stairway to street level. "Since I started so late, I need more practice."

CHAPTER 8
LIZZY

MASON WHISTLES as he stands on my front porch while I fish the key out of my purse. "This is nice."

"I love everything about it." I saved up for years to put a down payment on a house, and as soon as this one went up for sale, I knew I had to have it. "This was my dream house."

It's a small cottage home with a wraparound front porch, perfect for sipping tea or something stronger on a hot summer day. The exterior is painted a moody dark gray, which contrasts nicely with my aqua front door.

"This would cost a fortune in Chicago."

"Are there houses like this downtown?" I ask as I slip the key into the lock and turn.

Mason chuckles. "Not like this, but there are houses, mostly attached. You have to go a little farther out for freestanding units to become the norm."

"Do they have gardens? I love flowers. All the concrete in Chicago makes me itchy sometimes."

Mason places his hand on the small of my back as I push open the front door. "They do, and if they didn't, I'd make one for you."

I warm at his words, believing he'd do whatever it took to give me my dream. That's another thing about him. Something else that makes it hard for my brain to keep telling my heart no.

"Prepare yourself," I warn him as I take a step into the foyer. "The inside is more colorful than the out."

"I can't wait," he says, following me and freezing once he's fully through the door. "What the…"

I look over my shoulder at his beautiful face, his mouth gaping open and his eyes wide as saucers. "I told you."

"This is…" He slowly glances around, soaking in the few rooms he can see from the foyer. "Wow."

"It can be a little much."

For the last five years, I've put my personal touches on every single spot I can get my hands on. Vibrant colors to cancel out the dreary winter weather when sunshine is practically nonexistent. Striking floral wallpaper on areas I couldn't get perfect, no matter how many times I worked on the drywall. The wide-plank wooden floors are a rich, warm tone that flow throughout the entire house.

"No," he whispers as he wraps his arm around my middle, his front pressing against my back. He brings his mouth close to my ear. "It's perfect because it's you."

I put my hand on his as it rests on my stomach, loving the feel of him so close to me. The resolve I had to stay strong and not fall for Mason is slipping at an alarmingly rapid clip. "Thanks, Mase."

"I want to see more."

My belly flips for a second when my mind goes to dirty places. "I'll show you everything." My voice comes out huskier than I wanted.

"Lead the way, sweetheart." When he drops his hand from around me, I instantly miss the contact.

I set my purse on the side table near the door. "The dining room and the den."

"A den is fancy."

I chuckle. "It's not, but I didn't need a front room."

"Man, I haven't heard that word in forever."

"Your family doesn't have one?" I ask.

He walks into the den and runs his finger along the spines of the books on my bookcases. "Did you read all of these?"

I nod. "They're more than decoration."

"You know my aunt is an author, right?"

"I know. I try not to fangirl every time I talk to her."

He turns his head toward me and smiles, making my heart melt a little more. "Have you read her books?" He waggles his eyebrows.

My face heats, but I ignore the feeling. "Of course." I walk in and move to the romance section of my bookcase where her books are, which is most of my collection.

"Me too," he says and winks at me.

I don't know why I'm surprised. I shouldn't be by anything he does anymore. Plus, if my aunt were a popular author, I'd have to see what all the hype was about. "Did you like them?" I hand him the one signed copy I purchased from her website a few years ago.

He takes the book and stares at it. "This is the one I read, and yes, I liked it. Who wouldn't?"

"A lot of people."

"They're idiots," he replies, flipping open the cover. "It's signed."

"I know." I chuckle. "I purchased it online years before I met her."

He hands me the book back, our fingers brushing against each other. "I'll get you a full set."

I don't move my hand away from his as quickly as I should. Our eyes are locked, and I'm taken back to the kiss near the waterfall. I shake my head to clear my thoughts and bring myself back to the moment. "No, I have them all. I don't need another set."

"But I know the author." I bet I'm not the first woman he's used that sentence on, but maybe I'm the first who knows he isn't lying.

"So do I," I say, leaning into his space and bringing my mouth way too close to his.

His brown eyes search mine, and I can see a war

inside them. "You'd better back up, or I won't be able to give you a house tour before we start practicing."

My gaze dips to his mouth, and my breath hitches as he licks his lips, taunting me. Everything inside me screams for me to launch myself into his arms, but somehow, I resist the urge. I take a step back and pull in a deep breath.

I see a flash of disappointment in his eyes before it disappears. "Show me the rest of the house."

It doesn't take long for me to show him the kitchen and living room since they're attached. It feels a little weird having him in my house, even though I've been to his place many times.

Most people in the family, Mason's sister included, think we've been sleeping together for months. When Hunter was shot, Mason became someone I could lean on, and we spent more and more time together, but we never did anything physical. At first, it was because I wasn't in the right headspace for anything, given that I wasn't sure my brother would survive. And after that, it was because I didn't think my heart could survive Mason.

"And the bedroom," he says, one eyebrow cocked.

"There are two. I'll show you the guest room and then my room."

"Am I sleeping in the guest room?" he asks.

A small part, and I mean a tiny sliver, wants to say yes, but it's been so long since I've curled up with someone. Mason was the last person to hold me all night, and I've never felt as safe as I did that night. "No, silly. You can sleep with me."

That answer puts a smile on his face, and he's unable to stand still. He reminds me of a little kid waiting in line at his favorite ice cream place as they make his cone.

"With clothes on," I add, waving my finger up and down his body.

His shoulders slump, and I bite back a giggle. "Top and bottoms?"

"Bottoms."

He nods. "I can do that."

"Didn't give you a choice," I reply as we walk toward my bedroom, figuring there's no point in showing him the guest room since he'll never stay in it. "Here's my favorite room in the house."

He squeezes through the doorway, purposely brushing against me as he moves. "It's gorgeous," he says, looking even bigger in the space.

My bedroom is fairly large, compared to the size of the house, but it's filled with an oversized dark-wood queen-size bed and other furniture. The walls are matte black with black velvet floor-length drapes on the windows.

"This is perfect for sleeping."

"The color is really calming."

"It's completely opposite of everything else."

"I can't have bright and vibrant when I'm trying to get good sleep."

He places his hand on the bed and gives it a push. "Soft."

"It's adjustable." I paid a fortune for the damn thing, but it's worth every single penny.

"I don't know how you ever get out of bed in the morning. I need a bedroom like this since I work late and need to sleep well after the sun comes up. I never thought about black walls and curtains. It's kind of like being outside at night."

I never thought of it that way, but he's right. If I added a few glow-in-the-dark stars on the ceiling, it would be a perfect replica. "We could make it happen next time I'm in town. We can spend a day redecorating your bedroom to give you the best sleep possible. Do you have a sound machine?"

"A sound what?"

I walk over to my nightstand and press that power button. The room fills with the sound of falling rain, followed by a slow roll of thunder.

He points at the machine. "I want that."

"I'll get you one."

He shakes his head. "I'll buy everything. You tell me what to get and when you'll help, and I'll have it all ready for us."

I smile, loving that he always seems so excited and down for anything I throw his way. But men…sheesh. How does he not know what a sound machine is, especially since he has a sister? I'd think he'd know a little bit more about girl things, but sometimes his level of cluelessness on topics is shocking.

"Next time I'm there, I can come in a day early."

"When's that?"

"In two weeks. I'll be there more as the wedding gets closer."

He crosses his arms, tilting his head. "If we replicate your bedroom, will you want to stay with me when you're in town?"

Cue belly flip. "Um," I mumble, completely thrown by the question. "I..."

Staying with Hunter isn't all it's cracked up to be. I never liked staying with him when he wasn't in a relationship, but now, he's even worse. They try to be quiet, but the walls aren't that thick and the soundproofing sucks. Add in the fact that Amira is there most times I am, and sharing a bed with a kid who kicks in her sleep is the absolute worst.

"Yeah. Maybe I will."

Mason claps his hands and rubs them together. "Then we're totally doing it."

I throw my head back and laugh at the amount of excitement on his face. "You'll do anything to get me into bed, won't you?"

He stalks forward, backing me up against the nightstand. "I'd move heaven and earth if I thought it would make you fall in love with me faster."

I swallow, staring up into his big brown eyes. I don't want to admit it to him, but a small part of me fell in love the moment I laid eyes on him. "Mason," I whisper as he moves his hand to my jaw, cradling my face gently in his palm.

His other hand lands on my hip, and he digs his fingertips into my plump skin. "I'd paint my place pink if you were in it all the time. Whatever you want, Lizzy, I'd do it."

"Kiss me," I say softly, barely able to believe I am uttering the words. But although we were kissing by the waterfall less than an hour ago, it feels like it's been forever. I want to taste him, to feel his lips against me.

Do not sleep with Mason Gallo.

Do not sleep with Mason Gallo.

Do not sleep with Mason Gallo.

I repeat the mantra to myself, because right now, sleeping with Mason Gallo would be a mistake. I'm not ready for it, and there would be no walking back from the type of emotional connection that would form between the two of us.

Mason digs his fingers into the back of my neck, tilting my head backward before his lips slam down on mine. He steals the air from my lungs as our mouths collide, and my body longs to feel him in every way possible.

He presses his front to mine, sliding his hand from my hip to my ass. I feel small against him. His large hands and frame would make damn near anyone feel tiny, and for that, I'm thankful.

Just like by the waterfall, the world melts away and

nothing else matters but this moment. Our breaths mingle, our lips and tongues searching for something that isn't there, but that doesn't mean we will stop trying.

I fumble with his shirt, sliding my fingers under the thin material until I find his warm skin. I graze his flesh as I move my hands to his back, gripping him like he could evaporate if I don't ground him to me.

There is no doubt in my mind that Mason is into me. Even without the needy moans spilling from his lips, the hard press of his cock against my belly tells me everything I need to know when it comes to his desire.

Do not sleep with Mason Gallo.

Do not sleep with Mason Gallo.

Do not sleep with Mason Gallo.

It has been almost a year since I've slept with someone, and that experience wasn't one that I want to remember, but being with him damn near traumatized me daily. I'd always loved my body and felt comfortable in my skin, until he ruined everything by the constant put-downs and comments. Thankfully, I came to my senses and ended things, but not before he could get in one final dig. *You're useless, and no one will love your pudgy thighs and thick middle. You're unlovable, Lizzy.*

I gasp as I pull away, remembering the hurtful words at the worst time.

"What's wrong?" Mason pants, staring at me like I just took away his favorite toy.

"I'm..."

"Don't say it," he says, like he can read my mind.

"But you—"

He shakes his head and moves back into my space. "Do you want me, Lizzy?"

I bite my lip, feeling the sting of tears in my eyes. "God, yes," I groan as he reaches out and brushes a finger down my cheek.

"Do you want me to stop?"

I shake my head. "No. I just…"

"You're the most beautiful woman I've ever seen," he says.

What the hell am I doing? Why am I letting an asshole from my past, someone with a below-average penis, on top of it all, ruin the best thing I've ever experienced in my entire life? I won't give him that power anymore. He doesn't merit it, and I want and deserve better.

"I'm sorry, I—" But I don't get the words out because Mason's mouth is on mine again, taking away every fear, doubt, and criticism I have about myself or his attraction to me.

CHAPTER 9
MASON

"HOW WAS MAYBERRY?" Zoey asks when I walk into the bar only an hour after I made it back to town from dropping Lizzy off.

"Mayberry? It's Star Falls."

She chuckles as she leans her hip against the bar, crossing her arms. "Old-people reference. Never mind. How was it?"

"Cute."

"You could live there cute?" She raises an eyebrow, staring at me.

"Haven't you been? Hunter is from there."

"Nope."

"You're missing out. They have the most beautiful waterfalls. But no, not cute enough to make me want to move away."

"Not even for Lizzy?"

I suck in air between my teeth as I rub the back of

my neck. "I don't know. I need to get my head on straight. Would you move there for Hunter if he asked?"

Her lips twist as she thinks about the question. It's not an easy one to answer for me, but I'm not the one getting married. "Maybe. Not when we first met, but now, yeah, probably."

"You'd be miserable."

"I can find joy wherever I am."

"You'd really move that far away from the family?"

She sighs. "Probably not. I can't imagine not being here and seeing everyone all the time. Speaking of which, back corner booth is waiting for you."

I turn toward the booth, but I already know who's there. Amelia waves at me like somehow I'd miss her in the crowd. Nino's at her side, along with Lulu, Tate, Brax, and their spouses. "Fuckin' great," I mutter.

"Everyone wants to hear how it went."

"It was a twenty-four-hour road trip."

"With Lizzy. Did you guys..." She waggles her eyebrows.

"No, and even if we did, I'm not talking about it with you."

"Party pooper," she whispers and places her hand on my shoulder. "I'm proud of you, though. Maybe you really are in this for the right reasons."

"I told you I am."

"You've said a lot of things you don't mean in the

past, cousin. But for the first time, I believe you mean it."

"Would you be my cousin and my sister-in-law?"

Her eyebrows furrow, and I know I've just made her head explode. "I don't have the brain power for that right now. The bar's too crowded. I have work to do, and as soon as you're done with those weirdos, you do too."

I lift my hands and back away, needing to get the talk over with my nosy-ass family. "Five minutes, and you've got me all night."

As I approach the booth, every set of eyes is on me. I wonder if they did a group chat on the side to plan their meeting here to discuss my love life. They're weird enough to do that.

Amelia sits up straighter as I get closer. "How was it? Are you two a thing now?" She's overly excited, but that's nothing new for my cousin.

She's said she's living vicariously through us until she finds a man to sweep her off her feet. I'm honestly shocked it hasn't happened yet because she's a good one. She's sweet, kind, beautiful, and although sometimes she can be a bit annoying because she's a people pleaser, it's coming from a good place.

I stand at the end of the table, feeling like I'm about to give a presentation instead of greeting my family. "Not a thing yet, and it was good."

"*Good* good or good?" my sister asks.

I stare at her, tilting my head. "What the hell is the difference?"

"If we need to explain that to you, then you have more problems than we imagined," Nino answers with a smirk. Asshole.

"It was good, and beyond that, I'm not telling you shit."

"The truck work okay?" Oliver asks, not caring about the gossip when it comes to my love life.

"Yeah. It's a beast. Thanks for that and taking care of her car." I broke every speed limit on the way home, testing the boundaries of the hemi engine with more horsepower than I've ever had in my entire life.

"Shame," he says with his arm slung around Lulu's shoulders. "Her car's a total loss."

It sucks for Lizzy too. It was only a year old, and now she needs to buy another one.

"That sucks so bad," Amelia says. "When does she come back?"

"She'll be back for the bachelorette party next weekend and then the wedding," I tell her.

Amelia smacks her forehead. "How could I forget that?"

"I got shit to do," I tell the entire table. "I don't have time to answer more questions right now."

"Does that mean you will later?" my sister Tate asks.

I shake my head. "Not a chance."

"You're really boring," she tells me.

"Later," I say, tapping my finger once on the table before striding away.

As soon as I'm back behind the bar, I pull out my phone and check my messages.

Lizzy: Thanks for everything. I had a great time.

I can't stop a smile from spreading across my face as I read her words. I quickly type out a reply so she doesn't think I'm ghosting her.

Me: Me too. Do you need a ride back on Friday?

Her reply is almost instant.

Lizzy: No, I'm going to fly.

Me: Tell me when your flight gets in, and I'll pick you up.

Lizzy: Six at Midway.

Me: I'll be there. Send me the list of everything I need to get for my bedroom too.

The sooner I get everything and redo both bedrooms at my place, the sooner she'll start staying with me. The goal is to have her in my bed, not the guest room, but I'll work up to that for as long as I need to to make her comfortable—and make her mine.

"What are you smiling about?" Zoey asks, trying to

look at my phone screen, but I quickly switch it off and jam it back into my pocket.

"Nothing," I mumble and walk away, heading toward a group of new customers at the other end of the bar.

A six-hour road trip isn't how I like to spend my day before coming in to work the closing shift, but the exhaustion will be worth it. The last twenty-four hours were better than I could've ever imagined.

At eleven, the door opens, and my parents walk in. I blink a few times, wondering if I'm seeing shit because this is late for them to be out. Mom waves, always excited to see me because I'm her favorite. Or at least I think I am, but Tate swears she's the chosen child.

"What are you two doing here?" I ask as they slide onto stools across the bar from me.

"We went to a movie and thought it would be nice to stop by for a drink," Dad answers as he places his hand over Mom's.

For two old people, they're still always touching each other like their relationship is new. They're couple goals for me. If they're this in love now, I can't imagine what they were like when they first started dating.

"It's late, though," I reply, resting my hands on the edge of the bar. "Like, way late."

Mom chuckles. "I do stay up sometimes, especially since I've cut back on my hours at the bakery. Amelia's been taking more and more shifts. Her baking skills are becoming quite good."

Amelia has the perfect attitude for my mom's shop. She's like a little ray of sunshine, just like my mom, but I wouldn't expect anything different because her parents are great people too.

"I'm glad to hear that, Mom. You deserve a break."

"Within the next year, I plan to retire completely and enjoy life a little. I just need to get Amelia prepared to fully step into my shoes."

I rock backward at the revelation. "What? Really?" Mom hasn't said a thing to me about retiring. I don't know why, but I still think of her as young. She's barely aged since I was a little kid and has a lot of years left to live.

Mom turns to Dad and smiles. "We want to spend the rest of our lives having more fun and traveling. You kids are all grown, and now it's our time to enjoy life a little more than we were able to."

Dad leans forward, brushing his lips against her cheek. "Whatever you want, you get."

Mom gives her attention back to me. "Mix me a martini, sweetie."

I stare at her with my mouth hanging open.

"Don't look so shocked. I do drink."

"But you usually have a glass of wine."

"I'm in my vodka era now. I want an espresso martini."

"It's eleven."

"And?" she asks with a pointed stare.

"The caffeine."

"Get the woman the martini, bud," Dad says. "We're not going to bed anytime soon."

Mom smirks as she looks over at him, and I damn near throw up all the contents of my stomach. "Stop. I don't want to know what you two are doing at all."

"Then make the drink and go back to work," Dad orders. "You wouldn't question any other customer, don't question the previous owner."

"Damn," I mutter and shake my head. "Got it. What do you want?"

"A beer. Whatever's on tap."

"Mom and Pop letting their hair down. Wild shit," I say before walking away from them.

"They're so cute," Zoey says to me, watching my parents from the other end of the bar.

"Mom wants an espresso martini."

Zoey's eyebrows rise. "At this hour?"

"I said the same thing, but Dad told me to zip it because they aren't going to sleep for hours."

Zoey sucks her lips into her mouth and giggles.

I point at her and glare. "Don't say it."

"They're gettin' freaky," she sings.

I groan. "I don't want to picture them having sex."

"How do you think you got here?" she asks me.

"Stop. Make the martini for her, please." Zoey makes the best martinis in the bar. Mine are always too heavy on the vodka and not enough on the other flavors.

"I hope I'm still having sex at their age," Zoey says as she grabs a martini glass from behind the bar.

"Stop talking," I tell her. "Old people don't have sex."

She laughs again. "They clearly do." She dips her head toward my parents, who are all up on each other like a couple of horny teenagers. "And they're not old. Do you think Grandma and Grandpa still do it?"

I nearly vomit in my mouth as I fill a pint for Dad with my favorite beer. "Jesus, Zoey. You don't know when to stop, do you?"

She doesn't look at me as she makes Mom's drink. "I'm asking an honest question. At what age does sex become obsolete?"

"I hope never. How awful would that be?"

"Then why wouldn't you want our grandparents to do it?"

"Because they're our grandparents," I grumble as I take the martini from her hand. "I don't need the mental image."

"It's pretty grim."

I leave her and her crappy questions behind. "Here we go." I set down their two drinks. "Anything else?"

"Nope, son. We're good," Dad says, holding Mom's hand.

"Thanks, sweetie. We won't need anything else. We have everything we need right here." She has a lovesick look on her face that makes me happy and nauseated at the same time.

I spend the next hour ignoring my parents as they make a spectacle of themselves at the bar. Regulars stop by to talk, missing my parents around as often as they were when they owned the place. My dad was known for his solid advice, living through some awful shit, which gave him a unique perspective.

When I finally get a break after midnight, I check my phone again.

Lizzy: I'm headed to bed. Text me in the morning. xoxo

Long-distance is shit. We're not even dating, and I hate everything about it. Yesterday was amazing. There wasn't a moment of the day I didn't like, and now, everything seems so hollow and bland. All I have to look forward to for the next few days are some text messages and maybe a phone call or two.

Luckily, the bar will keep me busy, and if I have time, I'll also get the bedroom finished. Maybe I can tempt her here to stay if I play my cards right.

CHAPTER 10
LIZZY

Mason: Flat or Matte?

I GIGGLE and shake my head, although no one is here to see me. Mason's going full steam ahead in redecorating his bedroom. I thought he was joking, but clearly, he wasn't.

Mason: I'm at the store now. I've got everything else ready to roll.

Me: Matte is best. It has no sheen and won't reflect any light.

Mason: Perfect. On it.

No other man has ever been so effortless to be around besides my brother. I never feel like I have to be someone I'm not around Mason. He's easy, but sometimes I pause and wonder if he's being his true self. If

I'm not pretending, maybe he's the one who is. That's my worry, at least, but every time we're with his family, he's the same man around them that he is around me, which tells me I'm being paranoid and silly.

Me: Are you waiting for me to paint?

Part of me wants him to say yes, but there's another part that doesn't, because painting can be tedious. Not for me, though. I'd paint a wall weekly if I could and it wouldn't land me in a mental ward. It's calming and a great way for me to work through my thoughts and release my stress.

Mason: Want me to? Or I can knock it out before you get here.

I stare at the screen, blinking a few times. I land in Chicago in less than forty-eight hours. That's not much time to paint and redecorate an entire bedroom, especially one the size of his.

Me: If you want to paint before I get there, go ahead. I'll do whatever you want, though.

Mason: Anything?

The question is followed by an emoji with a raised brow.

I so badly want to say yes. It's getting harder and harder to keep my hands to myself when I'm around him, especially after the heavy make-out session we had when he spent the night.

A woman my age doesn't typically stop herself, but I know how easily I can get attached, and I don't know if I'm ready for that type of commitment yet. Add in the fact that the man looks like he should be on one of his aunt's book covers and I'm a bit fluffy in most places, and I still can't think about him seeing me completely naked.

So, instead of feeding into his question, I decide to go another way.

Me: I'm great at hanging drapes.

I swear I can hear him mutter a slew of curses from here, although it's impossible.

Mason: Are you staying with me or your brother?

I push off the couch and head into my kitchen, needing something cold to drink to quench my thirst that has more to do with my libido than the actual dryness of my throat.

Mason: I'm redoing the guest room too, so no pressure.

The question is ridiculous. We already slept in the same bed before, and I can't imagine lying alone, knowing he was that close. One of us wouldn't make it through the night without switching beds.

Me: You.

I guzzle a glass of ice water as he types his reply. I hope I don't regret the decision to stay with him, but I'm sure Zoey and Hunter will have something to say about it.

Mason: I'll finish it all before you get here. I want to make sure you sleep as well here as you do at home.

When I close my eyes in my house, I can't hear a damn thing besides the crickets outside my window. In Chicago, everything is loud, including the night. Sirens ring out, and the train rumbles by. There's never a moment's peace, but somehow, I'm able to block it out and sleep.

There's a knock on my door, and I jump, forgetting that I was expecting Mandy. She's my oldest friend and has always been my partner in crime. She's the closest thing to family I have for miles and miles.

"Bitch, open up. It's cold out here." Mandy pounds again.

"Coming!" I yell out as I place my phone on the arm of the couch before I make my way to the foyer.

When I open the front door, Mandy's holding a bottle of our favorite Moscato.

She pushes past me and twirls around to face me as I close the door. "I thought you were going to leave me out there to freeze to death," she says dramatically, her entire body shaking like she walked through a blizzard.

"It's forty outside, Didi. It would take longer than a minute for you to freeze to death," I tell her, taking the bottle of chilled wine from her hand so she can take off her coat and…

I point at her feet and shake my head. "You're wearing sandals. You're such a weirdo."

Mandy kicks off her black plastic sandals and then wiggles her toes as she rocks back on her heels. "I can't be cooped up this many months. I need to let something be free and breathe. It was my tits or my feet."

I laugh at my best friend, but I totally understand how she feels. Winter is way too long, and all the clothes are too heavy.

I leave her and her bare feet in the foyer and head toward the kitchen, ready to pour us each a glass of wine. "You picked wisely. I've seen your tits, though. They're spectacular."

"Yours are pretty fucking great too, babe," she replies as she plops down on my couch sideways so she can watch me. "I'd kill for your rack."

I can't stop myself from looking down at them. The girls are all right. They sag more than I'd like, but that's because they're heavy. "You're ridiculous. Yours are far superior."

"Mine are small. They're barely a handful. But yours

—" she points at my chest and waggles her eyebrows "—those babies are luscious. Any man would die to hold those puppies every night."

I wrinkle my nose as I pour two glasses with barely any empty space at the top. "No one's holding my chest every night."

"That's because you're being silly. It sounds like this Mason guy really likes you, but you're totally cock-blocking him."

I don't know which conversation I hate more—my saggy tits or my inability to move forward with Mason.

I walk slowly, careful not to spill a drop. "I'm not cockblocking him," I tell her, saying each word slowly like somehow my voice is going to make the liquid jump out of the glass.

Mandy takes one from my hand and gives me a look like my mother used to give me when she thought I was out of my mind. "Lizzy."

"Mandy." I use the same tone she used when saying my name.

I take the seat next to her, putting my back against the throw pillow. She stares at me over the rim of her glass. "Did you sleep with him in Chicago this time?"

"No." I don't add any details as I down half the glass of wine, deciding I need the liquor in my veins sooner rather than later.

"Why not?"

I shrug and take a deep breath. "I'm scared."

"Jesus," she mutters as her forehead wrinkles.

Disappointment is clearly written all over her face. "Why?"

"He's beautiful, Didi. The man could have anyone he wanted."

"Okay." She nods, and I think I have her on my side until she says, "And he picked you, but you're still cockblocking him."

"It's complicated."

She curls her leg underneath her and gets more comfortable. She's preparing for a long conversation I don't really want to have. "What is?"

"He's going to be my family."

"He's not your family, though."

"Hunter's marrying Zoey, who's his cousin."

"Okay…and?" Mandy tilts her head. "I don't get it."

"Can you imagine if we date and break up, and then I have to see him the rest of my life?"

Mandy slow blinks, staring at me without speaking. Mandy's never silent, and when she is, it's time for me to worry.

"I don't want to ruin anything for Hunter."

Mandy's lips twist for a moment before she downs almost her entire glass of wine in one giant mouthful. She sets her glass down on the coffee table and then gives me her full attention. "Listen, asshole."

"Why are you my best friend?" I ask her.

She waves her hand. "You're not derailing me. Hunter's going on wife number two and has the cutest little girl."

"She is, isn't she?"

"Be quiet for a minute. Let me get this out."

I lift my hands, leaning back into the pillow. I ready myself for whatever dose of Mandy reality she plans on handing me.

"It's your time. Hunter's had his and is having it again. Stop worrying about what could be if things go bad and start focusing on all the things that could be if everything goes right."

"Mandy, I—"

My phone beeps, and Mandy's eyes move to where it is on the arm of the couch. "Is that him?"

"I don't know. Did you see me look?" I'm being a smartass. I know it's him. He has a different beep from everyone else.

Mandy crosses her arms as she tilts her head. "I know you gave him his own tone."

"How do you know that?"

"You give everyone their own tone."

Damn it. I hate that she knows me so well. It's hard to spend thirty-plus years of your life together and not know everything about the other person. I don't think we have a secret between us, and I usually love that about our relationship.

"Show me a picture of him."

"You haven't searched for him online yet?" I ask her, because Mandy is something of a super internet sleuth, especially when it comes to dating and men.

"No, but I will as soon as I get home if you don't

show me his picture right now. I'll dig up everything I can about him."

I'm not worried she'll find anything bad. Mason isn't that type of guy, and if he were, I would've already heard about it from Zoey or Hunter.

"Fine," I bite out as I reach back and grab my phone. I open my favorite social media app, finding the page for the bar.

I haven't found Mason's personal social media accounts, but that's not surprising since he's a man. But whoever runs social media for the bar makes sure to put him and Zoey front and center, which is smart because she's as stunning as he is handsome.

I scroll down, finding my favorite picture of him. "Here," I tell her, turning the phone in her direction.

Mandy's quick, snatching the phone from my grip before I have a chance to move. "Oh. My. God. He's..." She pulls the phone closer to her face. "Fucking fuckable."

I hang my head and hold back my laughter. Of course she'd think that. The girl's taste in men is spot-on, but she's always willing to put herself out there more than me.

"You're an idiot," she tells me as her fingers move against the screen.

"Are you zooming in?"

"Duh," she mutters, studying every single visible inch. "What the hell is wrong with you, Lizzy? This man is drop-dead gorgeous. Look at him. Rippling muscles. His ink is striking. Big brown eyes, full lips."

"Again, I don't want to mess anything up."

"For whom?"

"Hunter."

"Fuck him."

"Hey, that's my brother."

"I meant Mason. Fuck him, girl."

"No, you were talking about my brother. I always worry about him."

"It's not your job to worry about him. Stop that shit right now. You need to ride this man like he's a bronco on the beach at sunset."

I gawk at her, wondering once again why we're friends.

"Does this have to do with he who shall not be named?"

I sag against the pillow. "No."

"Liar," she shoots back. "Get that asshole out of your head. He was a narcissist, and he had a tiny dick too. He doesn't deserve to live rent-free in your brain for the rest of your life. If you don't act with Mason, you're going to regret it until your dying day."

"I'm staying with him this weekend," I tell her. Why? I don't know. I'm obviously a glutton for punishment.

Mandy climbs off the couch, taking her glass from the table and mine from my hands. "This requires more wine."

I don't say anything. I'm happy she's done lecturing me on my self-image and being a cockblocker—at least for a little while.

"You're going to sleep in his bed but not sleep *with* him?" she asks from the kitchen as she refills our glasses.

"Yes."

"Weirdo," she mutters as she turns back around with a glass in each hand. "You're not allowed to come back to Star Falls until you fuck him."

I take the glass from her hand, not replying to her ridiculous directive.

"Does he want to fuck you?"

"Uh, yeah," I whisper into the glass, unable to meet her eyes.

"Then do it, and don't worry about your brother's relationship with his new family."

The last two words drive a dagger into my heart. I'm his old family. His only family besides Amira. "And if we don't work out?" I ask her.

"Then you act like an adult and ignore each other at all family functions moving forward."

I snort, nearly choking on my wine. "That's being an adult?"

"It's how I handle people I don't like." She shrugs. "You're going to sleep with this man this weekend, and then I want all the details. I mean all of them."

"I can't…"

"Finish that, and then we're picking out all your

clothes for your trip. You're not wearing things like that."

I gaze down at my old college sweatshirt and leggings, both of which are spotless and broken-in. "What's wrong with this?"

"We're going to glam you up."

"Fuck me," I whisper.

"Exactly," she says with a wink.

CHAPTER 11
MASON

"HELLO?" Tate yells from somewhere in my place. "Where are you?"

I seriously need to take away her key. I never cared if she showed up unannounced, but with Lizzy now staying with me sometimes, I don't think she'd appreciate the unexpected company.

"In here." I make my way down the ladder, placing my paintbrush in the bucket.

Tate comes to a screeching halt in the doorway, and her mouth drops open. "What in the world are you doing?"

I wipe my forehead with the back of my hand. I forgot how much hard work painting is, but it's instantly rewarding. "What does it look like I'm doing?"

Her gaze moves around the room, soaking in every single inch, even though it's still a work in progress.

"Are you going goth and didn't tell me?"

"No."

My sister steps inside the bedroom and twirls in a circle. "But it's black."

"It'll help me sleep better since I work so late."

Her lips twist like she's working through something in her mind. "You think?"

"I want it to be like a cave."

"You've got that nailed. It's giving total cave vibes. What color are the drapes going to be?"

"Black."

Her gaze finally lands on me. "Will everything be black?"

"I'm going to put a large cream throw rug under the bed, so my feet don't have to touch the cold-ass hardwood as soon as I climb out of bed."

"Smart. Smart."

Tate makes herself at home, sitting on the edge of my bed like she used to do when she was little. "What made you do this?"

"It's how Lizzy has her bedroom."

She straightens as a smile spreads across her face. "Are you trying to lure her to your lair?"

"She's staying with me this weekend."

"Oh. This makes me so happy. Tell me more."

I drop down to the floor, needing a break from the up-and-down of the ladder. "Amira is staying with Hunter and Zoey this weekend. And usually, Lizzy shares a bed with Amira, which, as you know, isn't fun. So, I told her to stay with me."

One of Tate's dark eyebrows rises. "In your guest room?"

I shake my head as I pull up my knees, wrapping my arms around the front of my legs to stretch my back. "No. She'll stay in here with me."

"Finally, some movement. Where are you two at?"

"First base," I answer honestly. My sister knows everything about me. We've never kept things from each other. When I couldn't go to my parents about something, Tate was my go-to person. She was older and had more experience, and since she's a girl, she gave me advice my dumbass friends couldn't give me.

"I still can't believe that. You've never moved this slowly in your life, and by the way you two were snuggling up on each other after Hunter was shot, I would've thought you two were sleeping together."

"Well, you would've been wrong."

"Clearly," she mutters, sliding down the side of the bed to sit on the floor in front of me. "You love her, don't you?"

"I think so." I wince as I say the words. I've never uttered them to another soul besides members of my family. I was never one of those guys who told every girl I was with that I was in love with them.

"That's huge, baby brother," she whispers, and she has a genuine smile on her face. "I'm so happy for you."

"It's been hard, though. Her ex messed with her head pretty badly, so she thinks she isn't worthy of me."

Tate rubs her forehead and groans. "Why are some men such assholes, and why do we find it so easy to believe them?"

"I don't know, but I wish she didn't."

"What's her issue?"

"She thinks her body isn't slammin'."

"Sometimes I swear you were born in the nineties."

"Dad made me watch some old movies. I like that term."

"It's not the worst thing I've ever heard. So, you love her body, but she doesn't."

"She's comparing herself to me. I think she thinks I'm too in shape and that she isn't worthy of me."

"Well, you need to prove otherwise."

I slap my forehead dramatically. "Why didn't I think of that?"

"Jerk," she mumbles. "Every woman is insecure about her body at some point in her life. We can't help ourselves with the impossible beauty standards we see in magazines, movies, and social media. Be encouraging and make sure to let her know that you love every inch of her. Use words and not just actions. Her ex used his words, but over time, your praise will replace his venom. She'll eventually become more comfortable with her body."

"I can also start downing donuts like it's my life's blood."

"Would you do that?"

"I'd do anything."

"Well, I wouldn't go that far, but don't sit here and eat chicken and spinach all day like you wouldn't dare put anything else in your body."

I wrinkle my nose. "I can't eat that shit all day, every day. Pizza all the way."

"I know. I remember. You eat garbage and look like that." Tate waves her hand in my direction. "It's maddening. I'd kill to have a man's metabolism."

"Speaking of which, where are your man and my nieces?"

"At home. I was in the neighborhood doing some shopping and figured I'd drop by."

"That's it?"

Tate nods. "That's it. Just a big sister checking on her little brother. We never get time to talk alone like we used to, and I figured it was time."

"You're a busy mom and business owner."

"But I'm never too busy for you."

"Sometimes you are, but don't feel bad, life goes fast and you have a lot of moving parts."

Tate gives me a sad smile. "I think about that sometimes."

"What about it?"

"My mom was around my age when she passed away. I can't imagine that happening to me and leaving behind my little ones and Wylder."

"You're not going anywhere." I scoot closer to my sister and place my hand on her leg.

"She didn't think she was either," Tate whispers, her gaze barely meeting mine. Her eyes are swimming with unshed tears, and nothing I do or say can take away the pain of losing her mom at such a young age.

"Is there something you aren't telling me?" I ask, even though the very thought makes my stomach twist.

"No. I'm fine. Healthy as can be. Trust me, I go to the doctor too much because I'm paranoid I'll wind up with the same cancer and leave everyone behind."

My body deflates as I exhale. "Thank goodness for that."

"Life's too short to worry about things like whether my thighs are chunky. I'm sure Lizzy knows it too since she lost both her parents, but that asshole made her forget it."

"I'll do my best to make her realize exactly how amazing she is."

"You're going to spend the entire weekend together?"

I nod.

"I have faith in you."

"Well, that makes one of us," I tell her.

Tate smacks my arm, the sadness and heaviness of a moment ago gone. "I need you to work harder. I always thought our kids would be close in age, but you're dragging your feet."

I jerk my head back, staring at my sister. "I'm not ready to be a dad."

"I know, but the longer you take to settle down, the longer it'll be for that moment to actually happen."

"Can you imagine me as a dad?" I ask her, shaking my head. "I'd be awful."

My sister moves forward, taking my face in her hands. "You'll be a wonderful father, Mason. You're just like Dad, and he is the absolute best. You're kind, caring, attentive, and sweet. You're the best brother too."

"You probably say that to Brax too, don't you?"

Tate smirks. "I'd never do that."

"Liar."

"You have Hunter's blessing too," she says.

"What? You two have talked about us?"

"When we have downtime in the shop, yeah. He's all for your relationship. He wants his sister happy, and he sees the joy on her face when you're around."

"Huh," I mutter. "I didn't think he wanted us together."

"He does, and he's hoping she'll move to Chicago too."

"Her town is so cute, though. Her house is beautiful. It's a big ask."

"When you're in love, you don't care where you have to go to be with that person. Your home is with them."

"What if she wants me to go there?" I ask my sister.

One of us has to move and everyone expects it to be her, but she may ask me to be the one to make the sacrifice.

"Then you do it."

"Really?"

"I'll miss you, but yes, you go where she is and live the life you were meant to live."

"I can't do small towns. It's worse than the bar gossip. I felt like I was in an aquarium with everyone gawking at us."

"Do you want the girl or to be alone?"

"I want the girl."

"Then you go if she won't."

"But I have the bar."

"Zoey can run it alone. Maybe Nino will pitch in. It basically runs itself. Start a new bar, a new life, a new love."

"I'll think about it," I promise her, but I don't think I'm built for that small-town American life.

Tate glances at her watch. "Shit, I have to go. They're waiting for the groceries so we can have dessert."

"Dessert this late?"

"Is it ever too late for dessert?"

"Not really, but I live my life differently from you."

"Nah," she says, pushing herself up from the floor. "I like the room, by the way."

"Thanks, I have tonight and tomorrow to finish before she rolls into town. I'm picking her up from the airport."

"Keep me posted on how things go."

"You'll see her Saturday night at the bachelorette party. Maybe ask her yourself."

Tate's smile is immediate. "I already planned on it."

"Of course you did," I reply, following her out of my bedroom.

"Give Willow, Hazel, and Maddy a kiss for me, yeah?"

"They'll be jealous I came to see you without them."

"How about I take them for a day soon? Maybe to one of the museums or something."

Tate pops up on her toes and kisses my cheek. "They would love that. The girls are crazy about you. I don't know why, but they are."

"I let them have unlimited ice cream." I'm joking, of course, but it's not too far off from the truth. The three of them send sad doe eyes my way, and I cave, giving them whatever they want when they want it. I can't seem to find the word no in my vocabulary when I'm around them.

"That'll do it," she laughs, sliding on her boots. "Catch you later."

"Bye, sis."

"Bye, baby brother."

I stand, staring at the door as it closes behind her. This is a hard time of year for her. She's always so morose around the anniversary of her mother's death. I can't imagine the depth of that pain, even though I've witnessed it my entire life.

I take a deep breath, tipping my head back to stretch my neck before I stalk back into my bedroom, ready to finish painting.

I snap a few pictures and send them to Lizzy. I've accomplished a lot in a short amount of time, but with the clock ticking down to her flight, I don't have much of an option.

Lizzy: Wow. You've done so much.

Me: I want you to enjoy the weekend and not spend time working.

I debated how much to do, but in the end, I decided that doing it all before she got here would be best for both of us. With the wedding fast approaching and the bachelor and bachelorette parties this weekend, we'll probably be too busy or too hungover to get much accomplished. Add in the fact that I'm excited to sleep in a completely dark room, and I figured I might as well knock it out as soon as possible.

Zoey and Hunter aren't doing the typical parties either. Instead of a few days before the wedding, they're having them two weeks before, and there are no strippers for either of them. The guys are going to one restaurant and the girls to another to enjoy drinks and dinner. Afterward, we're going to meet up at a bar.

Old me would've protested, but new me is going to use the opportunity to drink the night away with Lizzy.

Lizzy: You're very thoughtful.

My phone beeps, and I switch out of her text and check my other messages. The group chat between my cousins and me has messages coming in fast and furious, which is normally the case when all seven of us are participating.

Zoey: I talked with Hunter, and we decided to rent two limo buses to take us around on Saturday. No one needs to be a DD. Everyone can party and enjoy themselves.

Nino: You're my favorite cousin.

Amelia: Awesome!

Brax: You're a liar, Nino.

Nino: I wouldn't lie about such a thing.

Tate: You lie about everything.

Lulu: I'm the favorite.

I roll my eyes at the ridiculousness, and obviously, Zoey ignores Nino and most of the comments.

Zoey: Meet outside the bar at 6 on Saturday. Don't be late.

Me: That last bit is for Nino.

Nino: Amelia's the one who's always late.

Amelia: Never.

Tate: Always.

Not a single one of us is known for our punctuality, but we sure as hell know how to have a good time, and this weekend will not be any different.

CHAPTER 12
LIZZY

I DON'T KNOW why I'm nervous. I feel like I'm in high school and I'm on the way to prom with a boy I'd pined over for months.

"I can't wait to show you how everything turned out." Mason glances over at me. "It's better than I expected."

"How did you sleep this morning?"

"The best I ever have in that room."

I smile at him, staring at his profile as he drives us back from the airport. "That's great news."

"Are you excited about this weekend?"

My stomach flips as soon as he asks the question. It's all I've been able to think about. I haven't had an entire week with Mason since we met. We've sprinkled in days here and there, but never multiple overnighters. And then there's the kiss. No, not just a kiss. Multiple kisses and some pretty heavy make-out sessions.

"Totally," I say, sounding like a Valley girl. I stare out the window, unable to meet his eyes. In my periphery, I can see him glancing at me every few seconds. "You?"

"I think tomorrow's going to be a good time."

"It'll be something."

I'm thankful Zoey and Hunter have opted to have an untraditional ending to their singledom. While strippers were a good time when I was younger, the older I get, the more absurd it feels to me to pay men to show off what they would be more than willing to offer every day for free.

"Hey," Mason says softly, touching my hand that rests on the console between us. "You okay?"

I glance his way, meeting his eyes. I tick my head toward the road, wanting him to keep his beautiful brown eyes trained on the highway. "I'm good. Great, really."

"You seem nervous."

I can't stop myself from letting a bubble of laughter escape. "A little."

"Why?"

"I don't know."

"Because you like me," he answers, teasing me, but he's not wrong and he knows it. "And I'm the best kisser you've ever known in your entire life."

"Duke wasn't bad," I reply, giving him the name of my seventh-grade boyfriend, whom I never locked lips with, but Mason doesn't need to know that.

His fingers tighten around mine. "You don't mean that. No one named Duke can be a good kisser."

"What makes you think you're the best?"

"Because of the little noises you made when we were on your couch."

My face instantly heats, and I don't need to look in the mirror to know I'm blushing harder than I have in my entire life. "I remember you making some pretty interesting noises too."

"That's because you are the best kisser I've ever been with, so…"

My body warms at his praise, even if it's bullshit. "You're a good liar, Mase."

"I'm not, though. I don't lie, and I wouldn't lie about something like that. I don't think I've ever been as turned on as I was that night in Star Falls."

If my body were able to, I bet it would melt into a puddle of goo on the front seat. I spent a lot of time this week thinking about Mason and sex. Way too much time than I'd ever admit to anyone, really. And I came to a decision. One that I agonized over, making myself question everything in my entire life. But my final decision was that if sex were to be on the table this weekend, I'd be okay with that. I wouldn't say no. I wouldn't turn him down. I am done playing things safe. It is time for me to be bold.

"Me too," I squeak out, my voice barely a whisper.

"I can feel the tension radiating off you, sweetheart. Relax. New topic. Are you hungry?"

"Yes," I reply quickly, loving that he's happy to move on. While my new plan is to be bold, I'm not ready to have sex right this minute or keep talking about it.

"Good. I know a great pizza joint near here. They have the best tavern-style."

"What's tavern-style?"

Mason glances at me like I have three heads. "You don't know what tavern-style is?"

"I know regular pizza and deep dish because Chicago, but I don't have a clue otherwise."

"That's a crime and a pity."

"You saw our selection of restaurants in Star Falls. When I'm in the mood for pizza, I order from Benito's. Is that tavern-style?"

"No. That's wood-fired."

"I'm so confused."

"I'll make you a pizza aficionado before the end of the month."

"I assume it's your favorite style? Why doesn't your bar serve tavern-style?"

"I don't know. We haven't changed much about the food since we took over."

"You should make it what you love."

"I may have to do that. But people love our pizza, so we'd have to make it an option instead of completely replacing what's already offered."

"Well, you're the boss. You can do whatever you want."

"True. You're so damn smart."

"And you need to work with your mom's bakery to start offering more desserts. Everyone loves desserts, and I hate to say it, but your options are way too limited."

"You mean you don't love a single scoop of vanilla or the prefrozen chocolate cake?"

Now it's my turn to look at him like he has three heads. "How do you have a mom who owns a bakery and you serve the worst desserts possible?"

"Vanilla ice cream is a classic. It's hardly the worst."

I turn my head and stare at him. "It's boring."

He nods. "That, it is. We used to sell her desserts, but then she wanted to slow down a bit, so we stopped. But now, Amelia is going to take over, so maybe we can ramp up again."

"Really? Amelia?"

I don't know why I can't picture her as stepping into his mother's shoes. Amelia has the people skills, overly friendly like most members of the family, but I never knew she was a baker.

"Mom has been teaching her everything she knows. I think Mom was hoping Tate, Brax, or I would take over one day, but while we love eating everything she makes, we're all shit bakers," he explains.

"I can't imagine Tate as anything other than a tattoo artist."

"Me either. Brax, Zoey, and I have the bar, even

though Brax has stepped back a little more over the last few years. He doesn't have the love for it like we do."

"What does he love?" I ask.

"Trading stocks," Mason says those words like they taste acidic. "He helps out when one of us needs time off, but he's barely at the bar anymore. It's working out for him, though. He's making money."

"Sometimes it's hard to do something you don't love," I tell him, thinking about my job.

"Are you happy with yours?"

"No," I answer honestly, "It's more stress than anything anymore."

"You should quit and come work at the bar with me."

He says it so casually, but right about now, I'm willing to say yes. The last week was awful at work. Sales have been steadily declining, and instead of corporate coming up with strategies to fix the problem, they spend all their time blaming all the other people within the company, who don't have the authority to make any real decisions.

"You're kidding, but I'd almost say yes."

He sits up a little straighter, glancing over at me again. "You would?"

I shrug. "Serving drinks sounds better than what I've been doing."

"You know, you could come in as a partner. You can buy out Brax's share, or you could come in as an employee. Whatever works best for you."

I suddenly realize he isn't kidding. "Whoa, buddy. I thought you were joking."

"No, babe. No jokes. No lies. If you hate your job and your family is here, there's no reason you shouldn't be here too. Plus, I'm here. You'll need to do something, and why do the stressful corporate shit when you can work at the bar with me?"

I never thought about working anywhere other than the corporate world, but the dream job I thought I'd eventually get never materialized. And at this point, I think it wouldn't be what I had hoped. It would be more stress with very few rewards.

"You make some valid points," I tell him as we pull into the parking lot of a bar that could be the sister to Hook & Hustle. "This place has the best pizza?"

"They do." He parks and turns off the engine. "You'll see why in a bit." He turns his body to face me, our fingers still connected. "I want you to really think about coming here and working at the bar. You can always try it and see if you like it before you decide."

I mentally go over all the things I'd need to do to make it a reality, and it's daunting. I have a home and my entire life in Star Falls. But Hunter was able to pick up and move, so there's really no reason I couldn't too.

"I'll think about it."

"We'll talk more about it over pizza. You already gave me two great business ideas for the bar, and I imagine you'd be able to offer a lot more. You'd be a huge asset to us."

"Is that all I am?" I ask, teasing him.

He releases my hand and reaches up, placing his fingers on my chin.

I swallow as I stare into his deep chocolate eyes. It's as if all the air has been sucked out of the car, leaving a vacuum in its wake. My chest rises and falls, the heaviness of the moment finally hitting me.

"You're more than that. You always have been. I want you here. I want you with me. I want you at the bar. I want this. I want this every single day of my life."

This man is laying it on thicker than his mother's cupcake frosting. And just like I do with the dessert, I'm eating it up.

"Okay," I whisper.

"Okay?" His eyebrows rise, and a smile spreads across his face. "Does that mean yes?"

"It means I'll think about it. Let's see how this weekend goes before I make a final decision."

"Will you decide by the time your flight leaves on Sunday?"

My mouth answers before I have a chance to process anything. "Yes."

Mason leans forward, and I hold my breath. My eyes search his, wondering if I'm leaping straight into the biggest mistake of my life. But when his lips touch mine, all doubt vanishes. Nothing has ever felt so right as when I'm with him. He makes me feel at peace, which is something I've never experienced before with anyone.

I melt into his kiss. All thoughts of pizza and the world outside disappear. There's only us. In this moment. Our mouths locked and our bodies wanting more. Mason's stomach rumbles, and the bubble we're in pops.

I pull back, needing to catch my breath and let my mind process everything. "We need to eat."

Mason doesn't back away, his gaze moving across my face. "We'll finish this later."

My toes curl inside my boots at the promise of more. "Okay." It's the only word I can get out without sounding like a phone sex operator because I'm so freaking turned on, I'm liable to climb over the middle console and straddle him.

A half hour and half a beer later, a pizza is set down in front of us. My mouth immediately waters. The crust is thin, and the cheese and toppings cover the entire thing.

"Damn, this smells amazing," Mason says to the waitress.

"Need anything else?"

"Another beer for her and a glass of water for me."

"I don't think I should…" I don't get the words out before he shakes his head.

"She'll have another."

"Two beers and pizza aren't the best way to end the night."

"Says who?"

"Me."

"You'll sleep better on a full belly."

I'll be bloated to high heaven, though. My gut is going to stick out from all the wheat and gluten, and I'll look like I swallowed a beach ball.

As soon as the waitress leaves, Mason places four pieces on my plate. Luckily, they're not the same size as a regular pizza pie, but damn. "Four?" I glance down at my plate and back up at him. "That's a little much."

"Shush," he tells me.

I rock back in my seat and blink a few times. "I may have to hit the gym this weekend if you feed me like this all the time."

"I go every day at two."

"Two in the morning?" My eyes widen, and I know I could never have that kind of dedication.

"No. I'm trying to fall asleep at that hour. I go in the afternoon after I wake up."

I still can't wrap my head around the fact his morning is my afternoon. I've tried working out in the early hours before work, but it only makes me dead on my feet by dinnertime. And after work, I'm also too tired and hungry from a very long day behind my desk.

"I could maybe go with you." In all honestly, watching this man lift weights would be completely worth the pain and misery of working out myself.

"Tomorrow?"

"Sure," I tell him as I pick up my first square-shaped slice. "Why not."

The pizza is, hands down, my favorite. I understand

why Mason loves it so much. There's no doughy crust, just a crisp, perfectly done bottom that does a better job putting the focus on the toppings than the other versions.

"That's the least enthusiastic acceptance I've ever had to an invitation, but I'll take it. Start small like the treadmill."

"Just don't put me on the stair machine."

He stares at me. "Hell no, you're not losing that ass."

My face heats again. "It could use some firming." I lift my beer, trying to swallow my embarrassment over my cellulite.

"Stop," he tells me. "You're perfect, Lizzy. If you want to come to the gym, come. If not, it's cool too. Don't do it for me, because I love every inch of your body. And if you give me the chance, I'll show you just how much."

I nearly choke on my beer. "You're so open."

"About sex?" he asks as he tilts his head and stares at me across the small table.

"Well, yeah."

"Not with everyone. Just you."

"Oh," I whisper.

"I take it you're not so open?"

I shake my head. "I was raised too Catholic for that."

Mason snorts. "Understood. So, have you thought more about my offer?"

"Which one?" There's the sex offer and then the business one.

"Moving here and working at the bar. You can tell your boss to go fuck himself."

God, I liked the sound of that. "There's so much that would have to be done."

"Your house will sell in a heartbeat. It's too damn pretty."

"Thanks." I've never imagined living anywhere else, but there's nothing left for me in Star Falls. Everything I want is here. Hunter, Amira, Mason, the entire Gallo family. They're my people, and work has become just that...work. "I need the weekend to think about it."

"I can talk to Brax for you if you want more details on possibly buying out his share. I'm sure he'd love to walk away from it all without giving you a huge price tag."

"You think?"

I don't want to get my hopes up, only for the asking price to be above anything I could ever come up with. I have savings and my house, but if he wants more than low six figures, there's no way I can swing it.

"Why don't you work at the bar for a while and see if you like it. If you do, then you can buy him out if you're comfortable. No need to jump in feetfirst."

"I never do," I tell him, reaching for another slice of the pizza in front of me. "I like that idea."

"Is that a yes, then?"

"It's a maybe." But there's really no decision to be

made except one. I'm not happy with my life anymore, and a change is needed.

"Fuck yeah," he says enthusiastically. "I'll take it."

CHAPTER 13
MASON

DID I JUMP THE GUN? Yes.

Do I regret it? Absolutely fucking not.

I've been this way my entire life. I act first and figure out the consequences later. Usually, I end up wanting to kick myself in the ass, but not this time.

"How much is it to rent a place in this building?" Lizzy asks as we walk into my apartment.

"A one-bedroom is a little over two thousand a month and probably another five hundred or so for parking."

Lizzy pales as she takes off her coat. "Are you serious?"

"Big city has a big price tag." I take her coat from her, placing it on a hook I hung near my door because I knew she'd be here.

I always thought my place was nice, but I realized it wasn't girled-up enough. I didn't have hooks or extra places for purses and whatever else they carry that I couldn't even imagine.

"I don't know if I can afford that."

"I have a spare room," I tell her, hoping she'll stay here whether we get into a relationship or not. At least, that's the lie I tell myself. It may be jumping the gun, but I'd rather her move in and be my girlfriend right off the bat. "You can always use it if you'd be more comfortable."

She turns, staring up at me. "What about someplace a little less expensive. Is that possible?"

"Why don't you stay here and save your money?"

She places her hands on my chest as she looks at me with her big doe eyes. "I haven't lived with anyone since I was in college. I don't think I'd be a good roommate at my age."

I reach up and wrap my hands around her arms, gently sliding them back and forth. "How about you stay here while you find a place, and if things work out, maybe you'll think about staying for good."

"Have you ever lived with anyone?"

I shake my head. "Always been on my own."

"So, what makes you think this would be a good idea?"

"I've never known peace like I feel when you're around."

"I don't talk a lot, so that's a given."

I chuckle at her ridiculousness. "That's not what I mean."

"I'm picky, Mason. I like everything a certain way. I think I'd make an awful roommate, and you'll be sick of me in a week."

"We have three days together to see how it would go. You don't need to give me an answer now, but it's an option."

I don't know what's come over me. A year ago, if someone would've told me I'd ask a woman—one I wanted to be with in a non-friend way—to live with me, I would've told them they had a screw loose.

"Why are you so great to me?" she whispers as we stand with only inches between us, staring into each other's eyes.

"Because you deserve it," I tell her.

Lizzy glances down, and I immediately move my fingers to her chin, forcing her to look into my eyes again.

"Never settle for less than this, Lizzy. If someone isn't going to be great to you, they don't deserve your time. Got me?"

Her eyes search mine like she's trying to decide if she agrees. "Yes," she squeaks out.

"No more dipshits."

"No more dipshits," she repeats.

"Now, do you wanna see my bedroom?" I waggle my eyebrows because, although I want to show her my redecorating, I also want to get her under me.

Lizzy giggles as her cheeks redden. "What do you want to show me so badly?"

"I have more than a few things, but I finished the room and want you to see it. I need to make sure it's right."

I added a couple more items than she had in her room, including a giant, full-length mirror near the bed. Last night, I fantasized more than a few times about fucking her and watching our reflection. But I can't think of that now or else I won't be able to walk right.

"Lead the way," she says, as if she hasn't been in my bedroom and doesn't know exactly where it is.

I take her hand, leading her toward my redecorated bedroom. This moment feels like I'm about to unveil my life's work to a discerning audience that'll make or break me.

Lizzy steps into the room, and I switch on the light.

She gasps and covers her mouth. "It's..." She doesn't finish the sentence.

My stomach flips, and I wonder if I got the wrong shade of black. Is that even a thing? Black is black, isn't it?

"It's stunning," she finally says before I have a chance to panic. "I can't believe you did all this so quickly."

I didn't have much else to do this week. I worked at the bar and spent all my other time finishing the bedroom.

"I was highly motivated."

Lizzy squeezes my fingers. "You did a few things differently, and it's better than my bedroom." Her gaze moves to the mirror, which has a chunky, dark-wood frame and leans against the wall. "That is a great addition. I could get a lot of use out of it."

I know I was hoping we would. If not this weekend, then soon. "I loved it as soon as I saw it."

Besides the small mirror above my sink, I never look at my own reflection. I don't need to, but I have other reasons, sexy ones, to put one in my bedroom in the perfect place to get a great view from the bed.

"So, you'd sleep in here?"

"I could live in this room." She points to a black velvet chaise I added to the corner near the window. "That's a perfect spot to curl up with a book."

I don't want to tell her that I thought of her when I bought it and put it there. I pictured her doing just that, curling up with a book and a blanket, spending hours devouring pages.

"We just need to get a few bookcases, and you'll be all set."

"You've really thought of everything, haven't you?"

"I tried."

"You did," she tells me and spins around to face me. "I'm impressed."

"I'm a motivated man," I answer honestly. I'd had the same paint color on the walls that was here when I moved in. I never once thought about changing it until I saw her bedroom. And then there's the fact that I want her to stay with me.

She steps forward, eliminating the little bit of

distance between us. "You impress me," she whispers. "This was so sweet."

I don't want to tell her I did it for me too. I spent way too many years getting shit sleep and having the sun wake me up hours earlier than I wanted.

"I'd do anything for you," I tell her, snaking my arms around her and pulling her closer.

She tips her head back, her eyes searching mine in the soft glow of the warm white lightbulbs she told me to buy for my bedside table lamps. "Anything?" She raises an eyebrow like I have limits.

She doesn't know me well enough yet to realize I have no limits when it comes to getting what or who I want, and right now, that's her.

"Anything," I say in a gravelly voice, ready to drop to my feet and worship her body. "What can I do?"

Lizzy bites her lip, and I can't stop myself from staring. My body reacts, my cock instantly growing.

"I made a promise to myself," she whispers, leaning her chest against mine. "I wouldn't stop myself from experiencing something wonderful this weekend."

"Like?" I want to hear her say the words.

"I want to be with you. I want to touch you. I want to see you."

"Same," I breathe out, wanting it more than anything I've wanted in a long time. My body aches for her. I've done my best to scratch that itch, but it's not the same.

Lizzy pops up on her toes and plants her lips against

mine. Her lips are soft, but the kiss is not. I tighten my arms around her, pulling her closer until there's no space between us.

"Fuck me, Mason," she whispers against my lips.

I moan at the thought, and I step forward, taking her with me as we move toward the bed. I've been dreaming of this moment, hoping I wouldn't have to wait too much longer. It is finally here. She asked, and nothing is going to stop me from making her wish come true.

I slide my fingers under her shirt and touch her back, groaning at her warmth and softness. The closer we get to the bed, the more frantic her kissing becomes and the quicker her fingers move.

She slides her hands under my shirt and lifts. "Off," she commands.

I like this bossy side of her. Not having to think about what she wants or if I'm going too far puts my mind at ease. I no longer need to think about what's okay or not.

I break the kiss, tearing my shirt off my body like it's on fire and I can't take another minute of the heat against my skin. "Just my shirt?" I ask.

But Lizzy doesn't answer. She's only staring. "Fuck, I forgot how beautiful you are," she says to me, her gaze trained on my abs.

"Babe, you've seen me shirtless before."

"But—" she waves her hand up and down toward my body "—I always tried not to look."

I don't call her out on the lie. I've seen the way her eyes drink me in every time I don't have my shirt on around her. "Take yours off," I tell her instead.

She swallows, and for a second, I think she's going to chicken out and get shy. I can see the doubt creeping across her face about her body.

I step back into her space, placing my hands at the hem of her shirt. "May I?" I ask.

She nods and raises her arms.

I pull her shirt up and over her head. As soon as I drop the material to the floor, I can't help but stare at her. "Fucking perfect," I tell her and lick my lips.

Her breasts are large, almost spilling out of her black lace bra. I don't even know how the thin material is keeping anything in place. Before I have a chance to say or do anything else, Lizzy launches herself at me.

I stagger back, catching her in my arms. Her warm skin meets my hot flesh, and I groan in satisfaction as I wrap my arms around her, holding her close and kissing her hard. We're frantic in our movements, working at each other's pants, trying to get naked as quickly as possible.

Maybe she's daydreamed about this moment as much as I have.

We're doing this. We're really doing this.

Our mouths part briefly as we strip off our bottoms, only to fuse back together with more force and desire than before.

"Condom," she breathes into my mouth, but I'm not ready for the main course.

"Not yet," I tell her as I push her down on the bed.

Her legs dangle off the side as she lands, and I fall to my knees and settle between her thighs. "First, I feast."

She gasps as my mouth finds the hot skin between her legs, and I get the first real taste of Lizzy. I dig my fingers into the softness of her hips as I explore her body with my tongue.

For a moment, I'm worried she'll push me away or become the shy body-conscious woman she has been. But just the opposite happens, and her legs fall open, giving me complete access to her entire body.

"You're so beautiful," I murmur against her skin, wanting her to know just how amazing she is. There's nowhere else I'd rather be than where I am right now.

"Don't talk," she says with rushed breaths, panting with each stroke of my tongue against her.

I smirk at her boldness, loving this new side of Lizzy. I close my lips around her clit, drawing it into my mouth as I flick it with my tongue. Her body rocks forward in a sudden movement, and I know I'm at the right spot.

She moves her hands to her breasts, toying with her nipples. I have the perfect view, straight up her body to where she's touching herself. If my cock weren't as stiff as a board before, it sure as fuck is now.

I press my fingers against her pussy, sliding them along both sides of my mouth. I coat them with my spit and Lizzy's wetness, needing to be inside her any way I can.

I'd dreamed of this moment. Fantasized about it for months. Jacked off to it more times than I can count, and now it's here. *Don't rush this, dumbass. Savor her. Savor this.*

I don't move my mouth from her core as I push a single finger inside her. She contracts around the digit, sucking me deeper. I slowly move it in and out a few times, building up for her to accept more. If she's going to take my cock, I need my girl to stretch a little. The last thing I want to do is make the experience painful for her.

I add a second finger and stroke her G-spot, knowing I've found it by the way her breathing changes and her body quakes. If she's like other women I know, she's been with a string of lousy lovers who didn't know a clit from a fold of skin. I want to blow this woman's mind, giving her the best orgasm of her life.

It doesn't take long before Lizzy's legs are straining with each swipe of my tongue across her clit. I concentrate, although it's hard with the way she's pulling on her nipples, and work the pad of my two fingers against her G-spot. I keep the strokes steady, careful not to go too fast or press too hard.

Lizzy cries out before my jaw even has a chance to get tired. She moans as her legs shake around my ears. Her beautiful pussy squeezes my fingers, holding them inside her as she rides the wave of an orgasm.

When her legs stop moving and her body goes bone-less, I feel a greater sense of pride than I've felt in a long time. Lizzy lies on the bed with her hands on her chest, her breathing heavy. "Fuck," she whispers.

I climb to my feet and lick my fingers as I stare down at the most beautiful woman my eyes have ever had the honor of looking at. "I'm doing that again. But first…" I place my wet fingers around my cock, and Lizzy's eyes follow.

"Shit," she mutters as she props herself up on her elbows. "You're… I don't know if…"

"It'll be fine, sweetheart. I'll go slow."

She swallows and then licks her lips. "I want to taste you."

"I need to be inside you first," I tell her, stroking my cock hard enough to give pleasure, but not too hard because I know I'll come too damn quick.

Lizzy pouts, and it's fucking adorable. "Condom," she reminds me. "Do you have one?"

"I got it," I tell her as I walk around the bed and grab one from the nightstand. When I turn back around, Lizzy's green eyes are trained on me.

She looks like an angel with her blond hair billowing over her shoulders and across her breasts. "I want you inside me," she says. "I need it."

"My baby needs more?" I ask, rolling the condom over my cock but wishing I could go bareback.

"I don't know if I'll ever get enough of you."

I place a knee on the bed before hooking my hands

under her arms. I push her body up the bed and crawl between her legs. My body covers hers as I stare down into her eyes. "You can have me anytime you want me. We have a lifetime to do this."

"Will that be enough?" she asks, her eyes twinkling in the faint glow of the room.

"I'm going to give you so many orgasms, you'll beg me to stop," I promise her as I hover above her.

"I'll never say those words."

"Challenge accepted," I tease, poking at her entrance with the head of my cock. "I'll go slow."

"Don't," she says. "I changed my mind. I don't want slow, Mason. Hard and fast."

I groan and take her mouth again, stroking my tongue against hers as I thrust inside her in one stroke. I pause when I'm fully seated, needing a minute to gather my scattered thoughts. But I don't have long to think because Lizzy digs her heels into my ass, and I know I need to get moving.

I love it hard and fast, but I haven't been inside another woman since the day I met Lizzy. I'm not going to last long, but hopefully she'll understand why and not think I'm a lousy lover.

I thrust in and out of her as I kiss her deeper and harder, matching the tempo of my cock. Lizzy moans as her body jerks underneath me.

She wraps both legs around me, sealing our bodies together and making it damn near impossible for me to pull out too far. I roll with it. I don't need to go wild, and being buried all the way inside her is more than enough to get me off.

It doesn't take long before I grunt through a few more thrusts, and an orgasm overtakes me. I'm unable to stop it, and all I can do is ride the wave of pleasure that overwhelms every sense and fiber in my body.

"Fuck. I'm sorry," I pant above her while I'm still buried deep. "That was too fast, but you got me all crazy."

"It was more than enough," she whispers, stroking my hair with her fingers.

"Sweetheart, it wasn't, but I'm going to make up for it while I rebound."

"Make up for it?" she asks as I crawl backward down her body. "Already?"

"I said I was going to give you a lot of orgasms. We're going for number two."

"Two in one night?" Her eyes are wide like she's never had two. Hell, maybe she's never had one from anyone else, and the thought of two is beyond her comprehension.

"No fewer than three before you go to sleep."

"Oh." Her mouth hangs open with her lips in a perfect O.

"Lie back and spread wide, baby," I tell her as I find my spot on the floor and gaze at what's mine.

She does as she's told, opening her legs. "Touch yourself," I tell her. "Play with your breasts. I like to watch while I eat."

Lizzy lifts a hand without argument, finding the nipple of her right breast. Her fingertips pluck at the tip and pinch. Fuck, I have to remember she likes her nipples played with roughly. I'd add it to my arsenal to use later.

"We're going slower this time," I tell her before my mouth finds the spot. I could spend a lifetime like this, and if I have my way, I will.

CHAPTER 14
LIZZY

"YOU'RE GLOWING," Tilly, Mason's mom, says across from me as we finish dinner.

I cough, nearly choking on my martini. I don't need to look in a mirror to know my face is turning red.

"That's because they finally did it," Tate tells Tilly, like they're talking about us going for a walk and not sleeping together.

Mortification isn't a strong enough word. If I could crawl into a hole and disappear forever, I would.

Tilly's face doesn't change. Her smile stays where it was, and she appears to be unfazed by the salacious news. "Are you two a couple finally? Please say you are. I couldn't think of a better woman for my son."

I don't know what to do with that statement. The few times I'd met the mother of the man I was dating, they always acted like I was stealing their grown-ass child or I would somehow morally corrupt them.

"I… We…" I stammer, unsure how to answer.

We don't have a definition of what we are to each other.

"They're moving in together," Tate answers for me again.

I turn my head, glaring at her.

Tate beams, unbothered by my best angry face. "Chill, blondie. We've all been waiting for this day."

"How do you know all this?" I ask.

"There are no secrets in this family," she replies as she picks up her espresso martini that's nearly drained.

"Obviously," I mutter to myself.

I told Zoey what happened, thinking she'd keep the news to herself, but of course, I was wrong.

"We're all so happy for you two," Tate says.

"Beyond happy," Tilly adds. "A woman can never have too many daughters."

Her words make my heart squeeze with a mix of happiness and sorrow. I've felt lost since my parents died. Almost like I no longer had a home, twisting in the wind with no one to tether me to this world. The very thought of becoming part of another family and having parents, even if not by blood, has my body craving that life more than I want to admit.

"We're not getting married," I say.

Tilly strokes her long braid that hangs down one side of her head and over her chest. "You became part of this family the moment your brother and Zoey got together, but now…" Tilly tilts her head as she smiles at me with calming joy. "Now, you are part of my family too, and I don't need a piece of paper or a priest to make that a fact, baby."

"You have two sisters and another brother now," Tate says, like this isn't weird.

I love the idea of having sisters. Growing up with Hunter was fine, but I craved some girl time to do girl things. I wanted to do our makeup, share clothes, talk about boys, and everything else sisters did together, but I never had the chance.

"We're taking things slow," I blurt out, overwhelmed by the outpouring of love and support.

"That's smart," Tilly says. "Nothing wrong with slow."

"There isn't?" I ask, because she seems ready to vault us into the future.

"Nope. Angelo and I took things slow at first, but there was no one else for us. We figured there wasn't any point in dragging our feet when destiny was pulling us forward."

I remember the first time I laid eyes on Mason. I knew I wanted him, but I never dreamed it could become a reality. He seemed out of my league and didn't look like he was the type that was ready to settle down.

"Mom, you always sound like a greeting card," Tate says against the rim of her martini before polishing off the last sip.

"I'm just happy, sweetie. All of my children are in love and happy. What could make a mom happier?"

"Grandbabies," Tate mutters. "More grandbabies."

"Now you're speaking my language. I could never have enough."

"Don't look at me." I raise my hands, knowing I'm not ready for children anytime soon. "We're too new and haven't talked about anything more than living together."

Lulu gasps. "Did I hear you say you were going to live with Mason?"

Tate laughs and shakes her head. "Lou, give it up. She knows we *all* know."

Lulu's shoulders sag, and her face morphs as her wide smile vanishes. "Why would you tell her? You're going to scare her away," Lulu says to Tate.

"She's not new to the family. She knows we're all gossips," Tate explains.

I did know that, but I hadn't realized how quickly news spread and how public it would be.

"We're happy for you," Lulu tells me. "Mason's a great guy, but we're excited to have you officially as part of the family."

Everyone is acting like we're getting married. It's odd, but it still makes me warm inside. I don't think I've ever felt so welcomed by any group of people for simply dating someone they're related to.

"Thanks. He is one of the good ones," I reply,

wishing I had another martini because this conversation is a little too personal for my midwestern upbringing.

Lulu pushes back her seat and stands, picking up her empty martini glass and a fork. She gently taps the side, and for a moment, I think she's going to shatter it. "The guys are at the Hook & Hustle. They're waiting for us. So, finish up your food and drink, and then we're leaving," she announces to the ridiculously long table of women who didn't stop talking to listen to her announcement.

I am excited to see Mason again. We've only been apart for a few hours, but this morning and afternoon went better than last night. Being around him is easy. He brought me coffee in bed, refusing to let me get up and make my own. I downed the entire cup while I read a book, and he cooked a large breakfast to fuel us for the day. And, man, I needed the energy because he didn't let me out of the bedroom until it was time to get ready for tonight.

"Cousin and sister," Zoey says as she throws her arms around me. "I love you."

She's drunk, but she's supposed to be. It's the last hurrah before her big day. "Love you too," I tell her, hugging her back.

There isn't a single person in this family I don't like. It's such an odd thing too. People typically aren't my thing. I'm a loner and always have been. I prefer a night in with a great book and a glass of wine over going to a bar to drink with friends. But this family has a way of sucking you in and never letting go.

"Will you be my sister or my cousin?" Zoey slurs, hanging on me.

"This is a weird conversation," Tate says, eyeing Zoey before smacking her arm. "She's your sister-in-law before anything else."

Zoey giggles. "Okie dokie," she mutters.

"You clearly need some water before we meet the guys," Lulu says, taking her sister by the shoulders and leading her back to her chair.

"I can't remember the last time I saw Zoey drunk," Tate tells me. "It's been ages."

"She's under a lot of stress," I say.

"It's nice to see her so happy again," Tilly adds. "The girl has been through it."

"Lulu too," Tate replies. "So Lizzy, when are you moving here permanently?"

That word makes my belly flutter. Is this forever? Is Chicago going to be my new home for the rest of my life?

"I need some time to put my house on the market and give my job notice." I have a mental checklist that's close to a mile long at this point. I need to get it down on paper, or I'll lose track and miss something important. "There's a lot to do."

"Do you have much to pack?"

I huff out a breath as I think about all my things.

Everything I've accumulated in my thirty-plus years of life. "Kind of."

"If you want any help, let us know. We can all come," Tilly offers.

I stare at her, blinking a few times. "You'd do that?"

Tilly nods. "Of course, sweetheart. Whatever you need, we'll be there."

"That's so nice of you."

"It's what family does for one another," she replies with the same kind smile that's always on her face.

"Okay, everyone," Lulu announces. "Let's go. The limo bus is waiting."

I am happy for the interruption of the conversation. I'm overwhelmed, not something I'm used to feeling very often in my life.

The ride to the bar is short. Maybe too short for many of us to sober up enough to last all night. I paced myself, only having one martini during dinner, and am saving all my drinking for my time with Mason at the Hook & Hustle.

The bar is jumping when we get there. All the men in the family are there and more, and the music is blasting with a hip-hop song I can't name but has to be making the glasses rattle.

I scan the crowd, looking for Mason, but come up blank. The women file in and go directly to their men, while I stand in the doorway, suddenly feeling out of place.

I stalk across the dining room and find Hunter,

who's holding on to a still very drunk Zoey as she peppers his face with kisses. "Where's Mason?" I yell in his ear loud enough for him to hear over the music.

He tips his head toward the back of the bar and mouths the words, "Back there."

I make my way around the bar, leaving everyone behind. "Mason," I call out, even though I know there's no way he can hear me over the beat. I glance around and see no one. I take two more steps and stop dead in the doorway to the office.

My heart sinks at what I see. Mason's back is to me, and he's holding the wrists of a beautiful woman as she sits on the desk and he stands between her legs. My eyes widen and immediately fill with tears. The woman looks at me, a smile spreading across her face as mine drains of color.

My feet move before Mason turns around. My heart races as I run down the short hallway, punching open the door in the back of the bar.

I'm an idiot. I thought he loved me, but we barely know each other. I knew Mason was a player. No single man who looks like him wouldn't be. But somehow, I convinced myself that he'd changed his ways because of me and for me.

You're delusional.

I'd let my heart be in charge instead of my head. I knew better, but I couldn't stop the freight train that was Mason Gallo from running right over me.

I run another twenty feet, stopping when everything

becomes too much, and my heart feels like it's going to burst through my chest. I bend over, placing my hands on my knees and let the tears fall to the gravel beneath my shoes.

This is what I was afraid of, and it took a total of twenty-four hours for it to happen. Record speed.

"Snap out of it," I tell myself. "He's only a boy."

But that's easier said than done. In the short amount of time we've been together, he made me feel like it was okay to dream. And what could've started as a fairy tale has quickly become a nightmare.

[illegible]
[illegible]
[illegible]

[illegible]
[illegible]
[illegible]
[illegible]
[illegible]
[illegible]
[illegible]
[illegible]

CHAPTER 15
MASON

"I THINK YOU'RE IN TROUBLE," Candy says as I push her arms away from me again.

"You need to leave," I tell her for the tenth time. I never put my hands on a woman, but she's refusing to leave the office or the party. "Lizzy will be here soon."

"I can't believe you're moving in with someone." She pouts, but it's bullshit. Candy hasn't dated a man since high school and is too in love with breasts to ever go back to dicks. "I thought we'd be single together forever."

"Well, you're going to have to deal with the fact that I'm leaving you in the game solo. I found the one for me."

"She's a stunner too." Candy waggles her eyebrows. "That sunshine hair and big tits are just…" She groans.

I sober a little. "How do you know what she looks like?"

"Like I said, you're in trouble."

"Candy," I growl. "What the fuck are you talking about?"

"She was here." Candy ticks her chin toward the doorway. "Stood right there and saw us."

"Fuck," I hiss and push myself away from Candy. "You're such an asshole."

Candy chuckles as I run into the hallway. I always knew Candy was a mean bitch. Her name makes her sound sweet, but there isn't a sweet bone in her body. She loves to play with people's feelings and watch the fallout afterward.

We were close in high school but have grown apart over the years. Though every now and then, she pops in to say hello and catch up. And unlucky for me, today was the day she strolled into the bar.

Fuck.

I glance both ways, debating where Lizzy went after she saw us together. I doubt she went back into the dining room and continued with the evening like nothing happened.

I make a beeline for the alley, hoping like hell she will be out here so I can explain. I can imagine the things flying around her pretty head right now. I could kill Candy for having the world's worst timing.

I slam open the door and rush outside. I look right and then left, finding Lizzy leaning against a car in the back lot.

"Lizzy," I call out as I run her way.

Her entire posture changes as soon as she hears my voice. Her back straightens. Her shoulders rise. Her jaw tightens and her lips flatten.

"It's not what you thought," I tell her, slowing my steps as I come nearer.

"Really?" She raises an eyebrow, crossing her arms over her chest. "It looked like you were holding a woman."

"If that's what you want to call her, but I wasn't holding her. I was stopping her." I so badly want to reach out and touch my girl, but I don't.

Her eyes are red, cheeks smeared with makeup from tears she shed over me. "Stopping her?" Lizzy scoffs as her lips curl. "Is that what you call what I saw?"

"She was trying to touch my hair, and I didn't want her to touch me. I asked her to leave, but Candy likes to play games."

"Candy," Lizzy whispers. "How fucking perfect."

"Sweetheart," I say, taking a step forward.

Lizzy juts out her arm, flattening her palm against my chest. "No closer."

"Baby."

Lizzy shakes her head. "I don't share, Mason, and from what I saw in there, you don't feel the same."

"Lizzy, Candy doesn't want me."

"But you want her."

I rock back and chuckle. "I've never wanted Candy. I've known her forever. We became friends in middle school."

"Um, that doesn't mean you two haven't—" Lizzy waggles her eyebrows "—you know."

I can't stop more laughter from bubbling out of me. "I don't have the right parts for that to happen."

Lizzy stares at me with her face all bunched up. "What the hell are you talking about?"

"Candy likes chicks. Always has, always will. She's had a thing for Zoey for over a decade, and when she heard she was getting married and about our party tonight, she thought she'd drop in and take one more shot. I tried to get her to leave, but the woman is stubborn."

"She likes Zoey?" Lizzy asks, her eyebrows drawn together, forming small lines between them.

"Uh, yeah. Totally into her tits."

Lizzy scrunches her nose. "You two haven't slept together."

"Never," I say, drawing out the word. "I swear. You can ask Zoey. She knows Candy all too well."

"How well?" Lizzy asks, quirking an eyebrow.

"Not in that way. Stop." I chuckle again. "Candy always shoots her shot and always walks away when Zoey turns her down."

"But you were between her legs."

Well, shit. She has me there, but I wasn't trying to get in Candy's pants. I'm not even attracted to Candy. The woman is pretty, but nothing about her personality would ever make me want to sleep with her. Even if she were into dudes.

"She was trying to wrestle me to the floor. She swears she's stronger than me. I wanted her to go. She wouldn't. She figured if she could wrestle me to the floor, she could lock me in the office and talk to my cousin without me interfering."

"Do you know how ridiculous this all sounds?"

I nod. "I do. God, I do, but I'm telling you the truth."

A moment later, Candy walks into the alley with Zoey at her side. "Hey," Zoey says, staggering a little before steadying herself on impossibly high heels. "What's wrong?" Zoey's gaze moves between Lizzy and me.

"Candy being Candy," I say to my cousin. "Lizzy thought she saw something she didn't."

Zoey turns an icy glare on Candy. "Tell her."

Candy sighs before she toys with the ends of her hair. "Fine. I don't like Mason. Nothing happened."

"And?" Zoey says, putting her hands on her hips as she sways.

"I like Zoey," Candy says softly. "I always have."

"You don't like penis. You never have," Zoey adds. "You almost ended their relationship because you're an asshole and like to fuck with people."

"I didn't do anything. I smiled. Is that a crime?" Candy shoots back.

"You knew what you were doing when you smiled," I tell her, shaking my head. "Now that Zoey's getting married, I don't know of any reason for you to ever come back here, Candy. Not after that shit you just pulled."

"Zoey's getting married, but Lizzy looks like fair game—unless you can't take the competition, Mason," Candy responds with a cocky smile as she gazes Lizzy's way.

"I prefer someone with a penis," Lizzy replies.

"I have a strap-on."

Zoey snorts but then lays into Candy. "I think it's time for you to say goodbye, Candy. You shot your shot and struck out twice. I've told you a million times over the years to fuck off, but you never seem to get it through your thick skull, and you won't be doing the same thing to Lizzy. You're banned from the Hook & Hustle going forward. Find another place to pester the female customers because you're no longer welcome here."

Candy kicks at the dirt. "Fine," she sighs. "You were never any fun and way too haughty for me. I prefer my women not to be stuck-up bitches."

"Off you go," I tell Candy, motioning for her to get moving.

She stomps away, lifting both arms in the air before throwing us her two middle fingers.

"Well," Zoey says when Candy finally rounds the building and disappears, "I'm going back to my party. You two good?"

Lizzy doesn't answer, so I do. "We need a few."

"Got it. Get your shit sorted. You two are meant to

be together. Lizzy, don't be too hard on him because of Candy. She's a bitch."

"I can tell," Lizzy says, giving my cousin a small smile. "We won't be long."

Before Zoey has a chance to make her way back inside, Lizzy walks my way. I open my arms, pulling her into an embrace. "I'm sorry," I say against her hair.

"You didn't do anything wrong. I jumped to conclusions," she says into my shirt.

"Shit happens."

She peers up at me with her big green eyes. "I should've given you a chance to explain what happened before I ran out of there."

"Nah. I would've done the same." I probably would've marched into the room and knocked a guy out if he was being handsy with her, but I don't want to tell her that.

"Will you forgive me?"

I smile down at the girl who captured my heart the very first time I laid eyes on her. "There's nothing to forgive."

"I didn't trust you."

"I think it has more to do with how you feel about yourself than trusting me, sweetheart. If the last twenty-four hours of worshipping your body haven't shown you how I feel, another twenty-four hours are required."

Her lips part as her eyes search mine. "I couldn't..."

"You can and you will," I tell her. "I don't want

there to be a single doubt when you get back on that plane."

"I don't know how I'm going to get on that plane if I can't walk right."

"Sounds like a good problem to have." I tilt my head, taking her mouth hard and fast. "Mine," I whisper against her lips as I inhale her moan.

"Yours," she breathes back.

We are okay. Everything is fine. We weathered our first storm. Even though everything could've quickly sunk, we were able to make it through.

A few minutes and a lot of kissing later, we're back inside the bar. My parents clock us as soon as we walk into the dining room.

"Everything okay?" Mom asks, always the first to see the slightest bit of change in mood.

"All good," I tell her with Lizzy tucked under my arm and her fingers tangled in my belt loop. "Just had to deal with some trash."

"You sure?" Mom asks again, her gaze moving between Lizzy and me.

"Yes, Mom."

"Baby, they're fine. Come on. Let's have a drink," Pop says to her. "Let the kids have fun."

Lizzy chuckles. "It's been a long time since I've been called a kid."

"When you have some of your own, you'll understand they'll forever be kids in your eyes," Pop explains. "When I look at Mason, I still see the little guy sitting on the bar, kicking his feet, and eating all of the cherries meant to be garnish for the drinks."

"Those were some good times," I tell him, remembering the countless hours I sat here as a little one and the thousands of cherries I consumed. "Funny enough, I now hate cherries."

"You ate a lifetime supply," Pop replies, setting his hand on my shoulder and squeezing.

Lizzy leans against me, placing her head near my shoulder. "I'd love to see pictures of him as a little boy."

That's all that needs to be said to make my mother's face light up. "Oh, I have albums and albums. Come over for brunch tomorrow, and I'll show you. We don't want to send you home with an empty belly."

I don't argue with my mom about already having plans tomorrow because it's pointless. Keeping Lizzy in bed all day wouldn't be a good enough excuse to miss having a meal with the family.

"I would love that," Lizzy replies with a big smile, and everything that happened earlier seems to be forgotten. "What can I bring?"

"Only you, darling," Mom replies. "We got the rest."

"Let's leave them be. They want to dance and drink and be young."

"I miss those days," Mom replies as she slides her arm around my father's middle.

"We're not old, baby," Pop tells her. "And I plan to…" He leans over and whispers something in her ear.

Mom leans back and gawks at my dad. "Tonight?" she whispers with her eyebrows high.

He nods with a wicked gleam in his eyes.

"Can you two not?" I blanch, repulsed and also impressed.

"Go," Pop says, ticking his head for us to get moving and leave them be.

"Come on, Lizzy. Let's leave the old folks to talk."

"I love them," she tells me as I lead her away from my parents and their dirty talk. "I hope we're like that someday."

"We will be," I tell her, and I'm hopeful that the words I'm saying are true.

"I need a martini," she announces as we get closer to the bar.

"What kind? I'll make it."

"Surprise me," she replies, placing her hand on my chest as she's tucked against my side. "Make it sweet."

I lean over, kissing her lips gently. "Your wish is my command."

I don't know when I became this corny, mushy guy, but I don't hate it. Not because I like the softer side of me, but because I like the look Lizzy gets when I'm that version of myself.

She makes me a better man.

CHAPTER 16
LIZZY

MASON'S PARENTS' house is damn near bursting at the seams when we walk in. I thought it would be just us plus Tate's and Brax's families, but I was wrong.

"Sweetie," Mason's grandma says, opening her arms before I have a chance to take off my coat.

I stop what I'm doing and give the woman a hug. She's so small, I'm worried I'd break something if I squeeze her with any force. "It's good to see you, Betty."

"Grandma or Nonna, please," she corrects before I have a chance to pull out of her embrace.

"We missed you last night," I tell her as I straighten.

"I can't stay up as late as you kids."

There's that word again. I don't hate it either. Although I know our parents loved us, they hadn't called us kids in years before they died. As soon as we were old enough, they treated us like adults. Part of me missed being doted on by them like we were when we were little.

"It was a late evening," I say as Mason takes my coat for me. I leave out the bit about how that wasn't the end of our night either. Mason kept me up for hours, making sure I had zero thoughts of Candy or any other woman taking him from me.

"Gimme a kiss, baby," she says to Mason, motioning for him to lean over to her level. He has a solid foot or more on her.

"Hey, Gram," he says with a smile on his lips as he curls forward to embrace her. "I'm glad you came today."

"Someone had to help your mother cook."

"Gram, let them in," Brax says, coming up behind her. "You need to learn to share."

"Can't teach an old dog new tricks, baby. If your grandpa didn't teach me, no one will."

Mason stares at her, confused by her statement. "Well, okay," he mutters.

"The man had a wandering eye and an even more wandering di—"

"Yep. That'll do it," Mason says, interrupting her before she can finish that statement.

Brax damn near loses it.

"Betty, I could use your help," their mom calls out across the living room, saving us from a discussion we didn't want to have.

"Got to go. Duty calls," Gram says, hobbling away with speed I didn't think she still had.

"That was crazy," Brax tells Mason, shaking his head. "Gramps really was a huge problem."

"Huge," Mason replies. "Thank goodness she stuck around, or none of us would be here."

"I couldn't. The woman is a saint," I say.

"Oh. She's not. Trust me," Mason tells me.

"Jesus," Tate mutters as she holds her head at Brax's side. "My head is killing me today."

"Too many drinks?" Brax asks, elbowing her gently. "Happens when you get old."

Tate glares daggers at Brax. "You want to say that again?"

"Not really," he mumbles.

"Didn't think so," she says, keeping her eyes on him. "Why are we standing in the foyer?"

Mason shrugs. "Gram ambushed us."

"Come in and warm up, Lizzy. I started a fire for us to curl up next to." Tate reaches out to take my hand. "Soon, it'll be too warm to enjoy the ambiance."

"I love a good fire," I say, glancing over my shoulder at Mason as I walk away with his sister.

Zoey's on a recliner, curled up in a ball. We're all feeling the aftereffects of last night, but no one more than her. She really let her hair down, and she has to be regretting it today.

"Why aren't you hungover?" Tate pulls me down to the floor in front of the fireplace.

"I only had two martinis."

With just one more day left in town, I didn't want to spend it sick, and I definitely didn't want to fly home with a massive headache and sick stomach. I'm not in my twenties anymore, and sadly, my recovery time isn't what it used to be.

"I had three, but man, I'm feeling it today. Thankfully, Maddox and Hazel are looking after Willow, giving me some time to get my shit together."

"Those girls are great."

"They're the best big sisters ever. They always steal her away to play. They fawn over her, which makes my heart happy. I love that all three of my girls are going to be close and have one another when they're older."

"It has to be a nice feeling."

"It is. My brothers and I are close. Brax and I used to do the same thing with Mason when he was little, but we were too young to be as helpful to my mom. I'm sure we gave them more headaches than anything." Tate chuckles as she picks up a glass of ginger ale from the extra-tall hearthstone.

The fireplace is massive, sitting off the floor by a foot, taking up nearly a third of the wall, and is flanked by windows. The house has dark, moody tones, the opposite of what I would've thought Tilly would've picked. She's so bubbly, but her home is not.

I loved my parents, but I would've given anything to grow up in a family like the Gallos. There never would've been a dull moment, and I can't imagine the words *I'm bored* would've ever come from my lips.

"Who are we talking about?" Iris, Brax's wife, says as she sits down next to us, facing out toward the family room. "Please tell me it's something good. I could use some gossip."

Tate taps her chin and twists her lips. "Did you hear about Timber?"

I've met Timber a few times. He's a solid guy and reminds me a lot of Hunter. The main difference is Timber seems to have his feet firmly planted in the single life, while I know my brother thrives in a relationship.

Iris leans closer, almost salivating to hear whatever Tate's about to divulge. "Tell me everything. That man is beautiful."

Tate rolls her eyes. "A woman came to the shop yesterday afternoon and told him she's pregnant and he's the daddy."

Iris sucks in a breath between her teeth, nearly hissing. "Oh, man."

"Dang," I mutter. "I can imagine that's not easy for either of them."

Tate nods. "I've never seen Timber's face turn as paper white as it did when she told him in front of everyone."

"That had to be shocking news," I say.

"Poor guy," Iris whispers.

"Poor girl too," Tate adds. "They're getting together today to talk."

"Have they been dating long?" I ask, clueless to the entire situation.

"I think they hooked up a few times, but nothing close to a relationship. Timber's never been into that life."

That's exactly the vibe I got from him. The man is a player with a capital P. Nailed it.

"As soon as you learn anything, you need to share," Iris rubs her hands together. "It's like a real-life soap opera. He must be a mess."

"He didn't talk much the rest of the day. I'm sure he's in a panic, but he'll work through it. There are worse things in the world than being a parent."

"Depends on the other person in the scenario. Did the woman seem okay?"

"She was definitely his type, but I don't know much more than that. She wasn't mad or upset. I'd say she was pretty level-headed, which is good," Tate explains.

"I just can't imagine," I whisper.

Brax sits down behind Iris and scoots closer until she's tucked between his legs. "What are we talking about?"

Tate explains everything again, and Brax looks as shell-shocked as Timber had to feel. "Fuck, that's rough."

"Maybe it's what is meant to happen to get Timber to settle down," Iris tells him.

Brax grabs a handful of Iris's hair and shifts it over her shoulder. "You think this will make Timber settle down?"

She turns her head, glancing at her husband. "Yeah. Of course."

"Wanna bet?" He smirks at her with a devilish gleam in his eyes.

"Laundry duty for a month," she offers.

Tate rubs her forehead. "You two are giving me a bigger headache."

"Zip it," Brax tells her before giving his full attention to Iris. "I was thinking something a little spicier."

"Like what? I'm not giving you my ass, baby."

The smallest bit of wind could've knocked me over after her response. My mind can't process the casual way they are talking about anal sex, and in front of his sister too.

"Fine. The loser isn't allowed to wear clothes inside the house for a month."

"Sweetie, all that nakedness isn't appropriate in front of Nova."

"She's a baby. She doesn't know any better."

"I'm not paying for therapy when she's older because we walked around naked in the house."

"Fine." His shoulders sag in defeat. "If I win, I get to tie you to the bed and have my way with you for an hour."

"No butt stuff," she repeats. "And if I win, I get a half hour foot rub every night for a month."

"That doesn't seem fair," he tells her as he rests his head on her shoulder.

"But it is," she replies. "Then I get one hour a week for a month with you tied to the bed."

She turns around again, staring at him for a minute before he says, "Fair enough."

Wylder drops down on the hearth next to Tate's ginger ale. "What's fair?" he asks.

"They're betting on Timber," Tate tells him, raising her arm and setting it on his leg. "Iris thinks Timber's going to settle down with his new baby mama, and Brax doesn't agree."

"I'm with Brax," Wylder says.

I look around the room, finding Mason across the way. As soon as our eyes meet, he waves me over. I don't say goodbye. I just uncurl my legs, leaving the conversation of Timber behind, along with Mason's siblings.

"You okay?" Mason asks as he wraps his warm arms around me.

"Perfect," I tell him honestly.

Every day I'm in Chicago with the Gallos is a great day. How could I not move here and be surrounded by this kind of love and acceptance? I'd be an idiot not to.

"Have you seen my brother?" I ask Mason as I peer up at him with my hands flat against his muscular back.

"He went to pick up Amira."

My little niece stole my heart the day she was born. She's had a choke hold on me ever since. The day I found out she'd be moving away felt the same as when I lost my parents. I grieved her absence, and my brother did too. The idea of living close to her again has me damn near giddy. When I'm in Ohio, all I do is think about being in Chicago, counting the days until I'm back here again.

"I love that girl," I tell him.

"She's a good one." He presses his warm lips to my forehead. "She loves being around the family."

"She's not the only one."

He smiles down at me, and my insides warm at the softness on his face. "They love you both too. You know that, right?"

I nod. "They're good at making everyone feel welcome."

"Not everyone." One corner of his mouth tips upward. "But when they love someone and make them part of the family, there isn't anything they wouldn't do for that person. Once you're in, you're in."

"We're both lucky."

And we are. Amira doesn't have any grandparents on either side, and before the Gallos, the circle was small. Just her mom, Hunter, and me. No kid should grow up without people to lavish them with love and kisses.

"The pictures are ready," Tilly announces. "Who wants to see old photos?"

Tate, Brax, Wylder, and Iris are the first to move. Mason and I follow them into the front room, a living room that's too small for the family to use when they're together. Scattered across the oval wooden coffee table are hundreds of pictures. Some are faded and small, and others are so large, they're meant to be hung on the wall.

I crumple to the floor, sitting next to Tate as I gaze across the memories. "Which one is you?" I ask as Mason stands behind me.

He reaches over my shoulder and picks up a photo with rounded edges that's torn in one corner. "That's me."

I take the photo from his hand, studying it. The little boy is damn cute with his shaggy dark brown hair and big brown eyes. He's wearing shorts and socks that are way too high up his shins, almost touching his knees. He has a football under one arm and is flexing the biceps on his other. His smile is large and infectious. "I wanted to be like my uncle."

"Why didn't you go into football, then?" I ask, running my finger over the faded paper.

"Tore my ACL sophomore year, and I knew I'd never get back to where I was. My dreams of being a professional like Uncle Vinnie died that day."

"What a shame," I whisper. But if he had become a huge star, traveling across the country to play, I prob- ably wouldn't have met him when I did, and I wouldn't be sitting here today. He had to give up his dream, but a small sliver of me is thankful for the accident.

"I didn't have the dedication it takes to become a

professional," he says, putting my mind at ease. He squeezes my shoulders. "I wouldn't change a thing. I love my life. I'm right where I want to be."

"Me too," I tell him, and I realize everything in my life has led me to this moment.

I hate that I lost my parents so young. That's the one thing I would change if I could. Would I be able to pick up and move if they were still alive? I'm not sure I could, but maybe they would move too in order to be closer to Amira. I like to think everything would have happened exactly the same way if they were still here, but I don't dwell on it too long because it's too depressing.

Never in my life have I thought about having kids, but being surrounded by this family and staring at the memories, I feel my body aching for something more. I want to someday look back over photos of my children when they were little and know I lived a full life.

CHAPTER 17
MASON

IT'S BEEN a busy afternoon at the bar. We were slammed for lunch, and the crowd didn't thin out until after three. The nights are usually busier, but luckily, I have the night off.

"Hey, man." Nino takes a seat at the bar, placing his phone and wallet down in front of him.

"Hey, cousin. What's up?"

"I wanted to check up on you."

"Me?" I scratch my head, staring at him. "Did something happen to me, and I don't know about it somehow?"

Nino chuckles and waves me off. "No, but I heard Lizzy's moving in with you. You're moving at lightning speed, and I want to make sure your head's on straight."

"It's straight as it's ever been."

On the outside, Lizzy and I are new, but we've been

close for months. I know her better than I've ever known any woman I've ever dated, and that includes Corinne, whom I dated for almost a year. The time I've spent with Lizzy has been quality time, talking nonstop, and not spent naked with nothing much more than moans and orgasms.

"You don't think it's a little soon?"

Nino's coming to me from a good place. One of caring and support. I'd be worried about him too if I thought he was rushing into something he didn't want.

"No, no. I want this. It was my idea. I've never been so sure about anything in my life."

Nino raises a single eyebrow. "Seriously?"

"Completely," I tell him, leaning over the bar in front of him. "Want a drink?"

"Just a soda. I have a date tonight."

"Oh yeah?" I ask, pushing off the bar to grab him a soda. "Anyone I know?"

"Not unless you know Starlight from the Amber Room."

"A stripper, man? For real?" I shake my head as I pull on the tap, filling a glass for him.

"You know cousin Thomas in Florida?"

I nod. "What about him?"

"Aunt Angel."

"What?" I stare at him and blink. "What about her?"

"She was a stripper."

"No shit," I mutter, shocked as hell as I set the soda down in front of him.

My aunt is stunning, but never in a million years would I have thought she was anything other than a receptionist. That's how I've always known her. She's worked at ALFA my entire life and somehow keeps the guys in line, and that's no easy feat.

He turns the cold glass in his hand, ignoring it while he starts to explain, "That's how they met. He was working undercover in a motorcycle club, and she was a stripper. I think her dad or some shit was in the club at some point too. I can't remember everything, but I know she danced."

"And what does that have to do with you and Starlight?"

"It's just a job, Mase. The woman's making bank, and if she's happy doing it, I'm not going to stop her. I'm secure in my masculinity. And her real name is Norah."

"Wow. You're more mature than most men."

"Well, they have tiny dicks, and I don't."

I laugh, loving my cousin and his confidence. "I hope you have a good time with Norah."

"I always do." He smirks as he finally lifts his glass to his mouth. "So, you're really good?"

"Couldn't be better."

He eyes me over the rim. "Okay."

"Okay," I repeat, hoping this line of questioning about my sanity when it comes to Lizzy is over.

"Fuck," Zoey hisses as she walks out of the back

with her phone on her shoulder, cheek holding it in place. "How is that possible?"

"Uh-oh," Nino mutters.

My sentiments exactly. The closer we get to her wedding day, the more stressed she's becoming.

Zoey tosses her phone down on the bar and groans.

"What's wrong?" I ask, leaning my hip against the bar and hoping like hell this doesn't turn into a full meltdown.

"My dress was shipped."

"That's good," Nino says.

Zoey laughs, but it's not a happy sound. "And they lost it."

"Fuck," I mutter.

"Exactly. They said it'll show up in time, but we have a week, and I need a final fitting." She buckles over, throwing her arms on the bar and plopping her body on top. "This is a mess."

"They'll find it," I assure her, hoping I'm right.

"Don't stores have hundreds of dresses?" Nino asks, stirring his drink for no good reason.

Zoey lifts her head, glaring at our cousin like he's a moron. Which he is. "They're samples and not for sale."

"Well, if they lost it, I'm sure they'll have to sell you the one off the rack."

Her glare doesn't lighten with his statement. "I don't want to wear a dress that's been on the body of hundreds of women."

"You're only going to wear it a few hours. I don't get what the big deal is," he replies.

Zoey straightens, and the stare she gives him turns icier, which I didn't think was possible. "Someday, when you're engaged, I want you to repeat that same dumbass sentence to your fiancée."

"Maybe he'll marry Starlight," I throw in for shits and giggles.

"Who the fuck is Starlight?" she asks, crossing her arms as she scrunches her face, but at least the glare has softened.

"My date," Nino tells her before he leans forward, taking an extra-long sip of his soda.

"A dancer down at the Amber Room," I add.

"Shocking," she mutters. "Of course you're dating a stripper."

He points a long finger at our cousin. "Hey, Norah's a nice girl. She's using the money to put herself through college."

Zoey lifts her hands and dips her chin. "I don't knock any woman for using what they've got to make a buck. If you're going to date a stripper, you'd better treat her right and not like she's for sale. Got me?"

"Yep," he pops. "Loud and clear."

"She takes enough bullshit from men every day at work. She doesn't need another one doing it to her when she's off," Zoey explains. "She's still just a girl with feelings and dreams."

"Got it," he says, ticking his chin at her. "I don't treat any woman like shit. They're all queens in my book."

I'm fascinated by the conversation. I don't know why, but I am. Not for nothing, but Zoey's worries about her dress seemed to have vanished for a few minutes.

The door to the bar opens, and Hunter stalks in, immediately lifting his shades onto his head when he's out of the sunlight.

Zoey squeals and runs his way. He doesn't know it yet, but he's about to get the tail end of this spiral about her wedding dress being lost with only a few days until the big day.

She crashes into him, wrapping her entire upper half around his body.

"What's wrong?" he says into her hair, stroking her with a gentleness Zoey always seems to need.

Before Hunter, she was a wild child, which led to bullshit she never deserved. It set her on a path that was grim, but somehow, he turned it all around.

"They lost my dress," she tells him, her voice pitchy and cracking.

"Baby, baby, baby," he whispers, running his hand down her back. "It'll all be okay."

"The man is a saint," Nino whispers, staring at their reflection in the wide mirror behind the bar.

"When you really love someone, you find the patience or they find the door," I tell him before stalking to the back to get my shit.

Hunter and I are going out tonight. Zoey's covering the bar, and Brax is even coming in for a few hours to help. It's all hands on deck this week with the wedding coming up.

An hour later, Hunter has calmed Zoey, and we are sitting a few blocks away at the best burger spot within a ten-mile radius. Spring training is in full swing and fills every screen on the walls.

I've ordered my regular. A triple patty smashburger with bacon and all the regular fixings, plus extra cheese. They also make their French fries in-house, and that shit is fire.

"How are you holding up?" I ask him.

He turns his beer bottle in his hands and lets out a loud sigh. "Good. Good. I wish things were going more smoothly for Zoey, but it'll all work out. No wedding is easy, and they all have their hiccups."

"In a week, it'll be over, and you guys will be on a beach."

"It can't come soon enough," he says, glancing up at the television.

"I've been to Nassau a few times. There's nothing like the water there."

"I've never been. Florida's the closest I've come," he replies, bringing his attention back to me.

"No comparison."

"So," he says, and I know we're about to get into the real reason he wanted to take me out tonight—Lizzy.

"My sister's going to stay with you. You sure about that?"

I nod. "She's stayed with me before."

"A weekend trip is nothing like having someone there forever, man."

"I know."

"She's not easy to live with. The woman is a clean freak and likes everything a certain way."

"I grew up in a house like that. My mother is very picky."

He eyes me. "It's different when it's your mom and not your girlfriend."

"Hunter, I love your sister. I don't care if I have to vacuum the floors three times a day, I'll do it. Whatever makes her happy."

"She said she might eventually get her own place. How will that make you feel if she decides to go that route?"

This feels more like a therapy session than a talk with my soon-to-be family member. "If that's what she wants to do, I'll support her decision. But with the price of rent in the city and our relationship, I don't think she'll want to be anywhere else. I fully expect her to make my place her home too. And if I'm honest, I plan to put a ring on that finger as soon as possible."

"Marriage?" He raises an eyebrow.

"Do I have your blessing?"

He lifts his hands. "I'm not her father or her keeper."

"I know, but do I?"

He smiles at me from across the table. "If you want to marry my sister, I can't think of a better man for her than you, Mason. I never thought I'd say those words, but I see the way you treat her and the way she looks at you. I know my sister is in good hands with you."

"Thanks, man."

"But—" he raises a finger, pointing it at me "—if you break her heart, I'm going to break your legs."

I sit back in the seat, staring at him. Is he serious? Would he really do that? Probably. I know I'd do that to someone if they hurt Tate in any way. I've given more than a few black eyes to some of her exes.

"I won't," I promise.

"Did you talk to Brax?" he asks.

I guess my response convinced him of my intentions when it comes to Lizzy since he's switched the topic.

"He's on board with selling his share to her if she wants it. She's going to work at the bar for a few months first to see if she likes it. It's a big change for her."

"Big," he says, blowing out a breath. "My sister's always been in the corporate world. I don't know what soured her to it all so badly, but she's burned out. I think this will be a good change for her, at least for a while, but I worry she'll miss the office life."

I wrinkle my nose at the very thought. "I think she's going to like the freedom of the bar. Your sister loves people, and there's nothing better than the Hook &

Hustle for that, especially the regulars. They're extra chatty."

"We'll see," he mumbles. "Besides a martini, I'm not sure she knows how to make any drinks."

I place a hand on my chest. "I'll make the drinks, and she can serve them. And she can learn the drinks over time. No one knows them all the first day on the job."

He leans back in his chair, crossing his arms over his chest. "You have an answer for everything, huh?"

"No, but I've put a lot of thought into everything when it comes to your sister. I know you all think I'm being impulsive, but I'm not. And I sure as hell know Lizzy doesn't have an impulsive bone in her body either. Does your sister do anything without a lot of thought?"

"No. Never," he mutters.

"Then, there's your answer. And if she hates the bar, there are a million companies in the city that would be damn lucky to have her as an employee."

He nods. "True."

"Now, let's talk about something more interesting." I rub my hands together. "You think we're going to win the pennant this year?"

"Hell no," Hunter says with certainty. "Cleveland's going to win."

"Hunter, brother, the last time they won, there wasn't even color television."

"It's our year," he insists with his chin raised.

"What do they always say? Maybe next year. It's your team's motto," I tease him.

"Yours isn't much better."

"My team beat yours for the championship ten years ago."

Hunter groans. "Before that, it had been over a hundred years since they won the big game. I hope it's another hundred too. How the hell did you grow up on the Southside but love the Northside team?"

I shrug. "There's something iconic about the stadium."

"Here we are," the waitress says, sliding two plates in front of us.

My mouth instantly waters at the sight of the perfect burger. "Thanks," I tell her.

"Anything else?" she asks, glancing between us.

"Another round," Hunter says, moving his index finger back and forth between our drinks.

"And a water," I add.

"Make that two," he says.

"Two beer and two waters. Coming right up," she says before walking away at a clipped pace.

The restaurant is packed, but I'd expect nothing less because their food is top-notch.

"Your sister has some great ideas for the food at the bar."

"Oh yeah?" he asks, his eyebrows raised.

"Yep." I grab the burger, studying it. "We're going to iron out some things once she's here, but we're going to focus on making the food better. Maybe we'll bring in bigger tickets."

"The food is already amazing," he says between bites.

"The menu hasn't changed since I was little. It needs a refresh."

"Don't get rid of the pizza," he tells me as I bite into my burger.

"Never," I mumble around a mouthful of food.

Some things are just as iconic as the city's baseball stadium, and that includes the pizza at the Hook & Hustle. It's our most-ordered item and a staple. It'll be on the menu as long as I own the place.

But I am more than ready for a shake-up, and I know Lizzy will help me do just that.

CHAPTER 18
LIZZY

I CAN'T LOOK AWAY. The movers I hired are working at warp speed. They've packed half my life away in boxes in less than two hours. It would've taken me weeks to do the same amount of work that they've knocked out in no time. They're worth every single penny.

Everything in my life is moving at a dizzying pace. I'm not used to so much change in a compact amount of time, but I'm rolling with it because I know what comes next is nothing but good.

My house is going on the market next week. I should have enough profit to purchase a majority of Brax's stake in the bar if I want. I haven't decided. It's a huge change for me, going from the corporate world to the bar life. While I love a great martini, I don't know if I'll like serving customers and working nontraditional hours.

I know my current life in Star Falls isn't bringing me joy anymore. I'm crossing my fingers that I'm not jumping the gun with both Mason and my career switch. All I know is that I needed something different. I want more out of life, and that is never going to happen if I stay in the pattern I've been in my entire life.

"Ma'am," one of the movers says, walking into the living room where I'm perched in my favorite reading chair. "We're done for the day, but we'll be back tomorrow morning to finish up."

"Thank you," I tell him.

The man isn't big on small talk. He doesn't say anything more as he rounds up his crew and exits. I take a few moments to soak in the sight before me. Boxes are piled everywhere, and furniture is covered in plastic wrap. Most of my things are headed to storage down the street from Mason's until I decide whether I'm going to stay with him. I'm not ready to let things go or integrate them into his place until I know for sure that I'm not making the biggest mistake of my life.

"You better not do this shit in Chicago," Mandy says, walking into my house. "You can't leave your door open or unlocked."

"Shit. The movers," I mutter as I cross the room to give my best friend a hug. "You're looking fabulous, as always."

She pulls back, looking me over. "Girl, you're practically glowing yourself. You're so in love."

"I am." I can't wipe the smile off my face when I let my mind drift to my hunky boyfriend.

Mandy looks around and whistles. "They got a lot done."

"I know." I sigh, happy that I didn't have to do all the work myself.

Mandy bumps my shoulder with her own. "I can't believe you're really doing it."

"I know." This is all so unlike me. I never leap into anything without thinking of the millions of little things that could go wrong.

"I'm really proud of you."

I turn to her, my chest aching at the thought of not being able to see her all the time. "I'm going to miss you."

"I'll come visit." She waves her hand at me. "No tears. We need martinis. Get your purse and shoes, and let's get the hell out of here before you turn on the waterworks."

"I'm fine." Of course, I'm lying. She's the only thing about the move that is tugging at my heart. Best friends are rare, and lifelong ones even more so.

"Bullshit," she mutters. "But you will be after a few drinks. We need to celebrate your fresh start."

I grab my purse and slip on my tennis shoes, ready to get out and experience my little town one more time as a resident and not a visitor. I've never lived anywhere else. I traveled a lot, but I've always had Star

Falls to come back to and call home. "I'm ready," I tell her, but I'm talking about more than drinks.

Ten minutes later, we're seated at the bar at Benito's. Although I'll miss the food here, Chicago has more than enough fabulous Italian restaurants to scratch any itch I get.

"So, tell me more about Mason." Mandy stirs her martini with the tiny straw spearing the blueberries. She opted for a lemon blueberry martini, while I went for a dark-chocolate one.

"I've told you a lot already."

"Does he give you the ick at all?"

I shake my head and laugh. "Not at all. I'm sure I'll find something when we're more comfortable with each other."

"The honeymoon phase will wear off eventually. It took a couple months before I found an ick for Tim."

Tim was Mandy's last boyfriend. They dated six months, but she ended it as soon as she found out he'd been cheating on her the entire time.

"But," she continues before I have a chance to reply, "I think, if he's the one, you won't have an ick. You'll love everything he does, even if it's bizarre."

"What do you think is something that's bizarre?"

"Bites his fingernails and spits them across the room."

"Ew, girl," I say as I scrunch up my face in disgust. "What type of men are you dating?"

"Losers."

"Obviously."

"What's the one thing you like most about him? I mean, besides his massive cock and muscles."

Thank God I wasn't taking a sip of my martini, because I would've choked. "He's sweet to me."

"Damn right. He'd better be. If a man isn't sweet when he says he loves you, you get the hell out. You hear me?"

"I learned that one already," I tell her, remembering the asshole who filled my mind with garbage. I turn my head, and my eyes land on that very person, as if I pulled him out of my thoughts. "Fuck," I hiss.

"What?"

"He's here."

"Who?" Mandy looks around and stops dead when her eyes find him too. "I'm going to kill him."

I grab her wrist as she starts to rise from her high-back chair. "No. I get to do this."

"Really? I can do it for you."

Mandy's always tried to protect me. While I try to be soft and sweet, she's always been loud and confrontational. It's why we work so well together. And while a lot of my kindness has worn off on her, none of her stronger traits have ever come out in me. Until now.

"I need to do this before I never see him again." That's one of the things I'm looking forward to in this move. I'll be leaving more good behind, but the little bit of bad in this small town will never touch me again. "I need to get this out."

"You do you. Just know, I've got your back if shit goes south."

"I know," I tell her as I slide off my chair and smooth out my clothes, standing up straighter and stronger than I ever have. "It'll only take a minute."

"If he does anything wrong, I'll kick his ass."

"Leave it to me, Mandy," I beg her. "It's my war to fight."

"I'll torture him forever after you leave, though. He'll never know a day's peace."

"I'm good with that."

She nods, and it's my cue.

I keep my eyes trained on Benjamin as I stalk toward him. My heels sound like the beat of a war drum against the tile as I lift my chin and prepare for battle.

"Benjamin." My voice does not waver as I stand over him, looking down at him like the tiny man he is.

His face lights up as soon as he turns his attention my way. "Lizzy." As usual, his gaze drops to my body, taking his sweet-ass time soaking me all in. "You look amazing."

He doesn't mean it. I've been sucked in by his smooth talk before. It's how I got myself into this head trip to begin with. He was nice at first, giving me compliments left and right, before he flipped a switch and made me feel like trash.

"I know," I tell him, and I truly believe the words coming out of my mouth. Mason has made me feel loved and drowned out every awful thing Ben has ever said to me. "But you're looking like shit. You feelin' okay?"

Ben clears his throat before placing his hand over the exposed skin. "I do?"

I nod. "Awful." I've never been one to be mean, but Ben deserves it. He doesn't care about anyone's feelings, and he sure as hell didn't give two flying fucks about mine. "Have you been sick?" I try to sound concerned and like I care, and even to my own ears, I'm doing a bang-up job.

"No." He glances to the mirror behind the bar, studying his reflection. "I've been fine."

"Huh," I mutter.

He pulls his head back, staring at me with his eyebrows drawn inward. "Huh, what?"

"I guess being an asshole has really taken a toll on your looks. Cruelty hasn't been good for you."

"Excuse me?" His eyes narrow as he processes my words.

"Being mean has made you ugly, or maybe you always were. But I never noticed because you made me feel like I was the ugly, unlovable one. But in reality, it was always you. Unattractive inside and out."

"How dare you," he seethes.

"I hope you find the relationship you deserve, Ben. I know I have."

I don't give him a chance to reply before I walk away, leaving my past behind me. Mandy's on her feet, clapping softly for me. I can't help but smile as my best friend makes me feel like a rock star. I refuse to allow people in my life anymore who don't lift me up.

"What's he doing?" I ask Mandy, not wanting to turn around.

"He stormed out." She chuckles and wraps me in a hug. "You still did it nicer than me. I would've added a knee to the balls before I left."

"That's hard to do with him sitting," I tell her as I wrap my arms around her and squeeze.

"I'm so stinking proud of you," she says as we release each other.

"Thank you. This calls for another drink."

"I like the way you think," she says as she slides back into her chair next to me and calls over the bartender. "One last drink together in Star Falls. The next will be in Chicago."

"When are you coming?" I ask her, hoping it's not months from now.

"I have a three-day weekend coming up. If you're settled in, I'll come then."

"I'll be settled," I tell her, not wanting to wait too long to see her again.

We're never gone more than a week without seeing each other, and that was usually because one of us was sick.

"I still can't believe you can't make it to Hunter's wedding," I add.

"I know." She slouches forward. "I hope he understands, but I can't be mad, because work is sending me to a conference in the Bahamas."

"My job only ever sent me to Detroit."

"I don't know how I got so lucky with such a great job," she says, pulling the two new martinis in front of us as soon as the bartender sets them down. "But I think you're luckier because you found love."

"Maybe you'll find it in the Bahamas."

She laughs. "Maybe I'll have a *How Stella Got Her Groove Back* moment."

"Wrong island," I say before taking a sip of my drink.

"Really?"

"Really," I tell her. "But that doesn't mean you can't have a whirlwind romance on a tropical island."

"The guys at the conference are always so…"

"That bad?"

She nods. "Maybe I'll be pleasantly surprised this time."

"You never know when love is going to find you," I say.

"Look at you. Who would've thought you'd fall for a bar owner in Chicago. A simple visit to your brother turned into your happily ever after."

"We haven't gotten there yet."

"You will," she says with so much confidence that I believe her. "If you didn't think it was going in that direction, you wouldn't be picking up your life and moving."

She's right. She always is when it comes to my relationships. I still remember the day I met Ben. Mandy said he was an asshole, but I didn't believe her. He was too good at hiding his true self from me, but Mandy saw right through his bullshit.

"I may not have met Mason, but based on the few video calls I've been on with you two, I can tell he's a good one. You know I'm never wrong about these things."

"I know. I learned to listen to your sixth sense."

Mandy lifts her martini glass between us. "A toast," she says, waiting for me to lift mine. As soon as I do, she continues, "To new beginnings. May you find all the happiness and love you deserve."

"You too, my friend," I tell her, clinking the glass against hers. "And a big cock."

Mandy snorts and brings the glass to her lips. "Life goals."

I'll miss this. I have Mason's cousins and sisters, and they come close to hanging out with Mandy. They are just as boisterous and funny, but we don't have the long history that Mandy and I do. Maybe that will change over time. At least, I hope it will. If I have my way, Mandy will fall head over heels for someone in Chicago and join me there so we can grow old together.

A girl can dream, right?

CHAPTER 19
MASON

Zoey: I'm freaking out.

Tate: Why?

Nino: Shocker.

Amelia: Oh boy.

THE FAMILY TEXT chat has become busier the closer we get to Zoey's big day. She had no fewer than three freak-outs a day this week. I'll be so damn happy when this weekend is behind us and Zoey starts acting more like herself.

Brax: Who do we have to beat up?

I roll my eyes. Of course, my brother instantly jumps to conclusions.

Zoey: They found my dress!

Thank God.

Zoey: I'm going to get my final fitting right now, and they promise it'll be ready tomorrow.

Nothing like cutting it close, but at least it's the one of her dreams. My cousin deserves everything to be perfect for her big day.

A message from Lizzy flashes on my screen.

Lizzy: I'm two hours out.

My heart pounds a little faster as I read her words. Today's the day everything changes. Lizzy's officially moving here and in with me.

I'm nervous as hell, but my excitement about all the possibilities outweighs everything.

Me: I'll be waiting.

I already am, but she doesn't need to know that. I go back to the family chat, needing to catch up. I missed more than a few messages in the brief minute I was away, and it is best to ignore them and pick up where they are now.

Tate: The bar is looking great.

Nino: I'm heading over now.

Amelia: It's about time.

Me: Do you need me?

Brax: No. Stay there and wait for Lizzy.

Lulu: All out-of-town guests have arrived.

Zoey: I'm so excited to see everyone.

That makes two of us. It's always nice to see the other side of the family. There are more of them than there are of us, and we're damn near not able to fit inside the bar anymore.

Nino: What time is the rehearsal?

Zoey: Church at 6 and dinner at 7.

Tate: Get your shit together, Nino.

Nino: Shut it, Tate. Where's the dinner?

Lulu: At the bar, dumbass.

Nino: Testy, testy.

Nino's in rare form and liable to be eaten alive by the women in the family if he keeps up the attitude throughout the weekend.

Me: We'll be there by six.

Today will be rushed. Lizzy will arrive, barely be

able to unpack anything before we have to get to the church to rehearse for the big day tomorrow. We won't have a moment to breathe until the wedding is over.

For the next two hours, I move things around, trying to find room for Lizzy to put her stuff. Luckily, I don't have much shit, which leaves plenty of room for hers.

She texts me when she is a few blocks away, and I go downstairs to wait for her.

My palms are sweating as nerves take over. I always play it cool like I'm not worried about shit, but if she's not happy and eventually wants to move out, it'll feel like a failure.

Lizzy pulls up in her rental SUV, which is packed to the top and almost bursting at the seams. She waves at me with the biggest smile on her face, instantly making all my anxiety over everything vanish.

I round the front of her car to open her door. She slides out, looking as beautiful as ever, even after a six-plus-hour car ride.

"I've missed you," I tell her, pulling her into a hug. I bury my face in her hair, inhaling the scent of lavender I've grown to love.

"Missed you too," she whispers back, hugging me tightly.

I don't want to let her go. I want to stay in this bubble of limitless possibilities, but we can't.

"We have a little over an hour until we have to leave," I tell her.

She pulls back, her eyes wide. "Shit. Really?"

I nod. "We can't miss the church part since we're in the wedding party."

"We've got to get moving," she says, suddenly in a panic.

I tick my head toward the doorway. "I brought a cart. We can get everything in one shot."

"Thank God," she breathes, clutching her chest. "We can do this." She nods, but not at me. It's a silent affirmation to herself.

"I got you, babe."

"I need thirty minutes to get ready."

"I'll grab your suitcase for you, and you can go upstairs and get ready while I unpack the car and park it around the corner."

"You'd do that?"

"Uh, yeah, babe. It's bare minimum."

"It is?" she asks.

"Fuck yeah."

"I thought it was more like princess treatment."

I shake my head, hating every douchebag she's ever dated. "Give me your keys. We'll have this talk later."

"What talk?" she asks as she places her keys in my hand.

"Expectations," I say as I head to the other end of the SUV and open the back. "You deserve to be treated like a princess every day."

"If you say so."

"I do," I grunt out as I haul her very large and extremely heavy suitcase out of the back. The wheels hit the pavement with a loud thud. "Jesus, is there a dead body in here?"

Lizzy chuckles, waving me off. "You should've seen me getting it in there."

"I don't know how you did it," I tell her as she curls her small fingers around the handle.

"Powerful thighs," she whispers to me as she leans in.

My stomach flips as I think about those thighs wrapped around my head. "Fuck. Stop. I can't show up at the church with a hard-on."

Lizzy grins. "Maybe we can fit in a quickie."

I growl. "Go. Move it. Hurry," I tell her, loving the sound of that, but the longer we stand out here, the less of a chance of that possibility occurring.

Lizzy chuckles as she walks away, hauling the suitcase behind her as she disappears through the revolving doors.

I unpack the car like the Tetris pro I am, getting everything on the cart with no extra room to spare. Rolling it inside is a little difficult because the damn thing has to weigh nearly five hundred pounds and the wheels aren't full of air.

"Sir, I'm sorry about the cart," my doorman, George, says as soon as I walk into the lobby.

"No worries, George. Can you watch this while I park her car?"

"Will you be using it soon?" he asks, rising from his seat behind his large desk filled with monitors.

"We're leaving here in an hour."

"Leave me the keys, but it can stay there. We don't have any big deliveries coming this afternoon."

"Really?" I could kiss the man. He's saving me a good fifteen minutes of driving around to find a spot on the street.

"Yes, sir."

George has worked here since I moved in. When he's not on duty, two men who are much younger and less helpful fill in the extra hours. I pay extra to live in a building with a doorman, but it's worth every penny when it comes to George.

I hand over the keys. "I owe you."

"You owe me nothing, sir. I'm happy to see Ms. Lizzy is here to stay."

"Me too, George. Me too."

He tips his head to me as he sets the keys down next to his keyboard. "Would you like help getting that up to your unit?"

"No. I got it. Thanks, though."

"See you in an hour. And, Mason?"

"Yeah?"

"Keep the cart up there until you come back down."

"I owe you bigger now," I say to him as I push the cart through the lobby to the waiting elevator. George is saving me the precious minutes I need to sate my hunger for Lizzy before we dash off to church to practice for the big day tomorrow.

Within twenty minutes, I have the cart unpacked,

with the boxes stacked up in the living room against an empty wall. They'll have to wait until Sunday, when we'll have time to get her more settled. All she needs for the next thirty-six hours are her clothes, shoes, and makeup to get through the wedding events.

The bathroom door opens when I get the last box stacked on top of the others. Lizzy pops her head out. "You ready?"

"To go?" I ask, suddenly stupid when I catch a glimpse of her naked reflection in the mirror.

Lizzy steps out, giving me a full view of her bare body. I nearly swallow my tongue at the lushness of her hips, heaviness of her breasts, and radiant flow of her creamy, flawless skin.

I stalk across the room, stripping off my clothes with each step until I'm as naked as she is. I grab her around the back of the neck, hauling her against me. I don't say anything as I lean in, taking her mouth against mine in a hard and fast kiss.

I move us toward the couch, keeping our mouths connected as we walk. This isn't about love. We don't have time for me to worship her the way I want to. This is about desire, a need that burns deep inside me to have my girl after being apart for nearly a week.

"Bend over the back," I tell her, wanting to fuck her from behind.

"Condom," she reminds me, but I am prepared.

"Got one," I tell her, reaching for the one I had tucked into the arm of the couch behind the pillow. I'd hoped this would happen, but even I'm not that good. I planted them in a few places, so I'd never be too far and we wouldn't have to stop for too long.

"You're too much," she says.

I dip my head toward the couch, and Lizzy understands exactly what I want. She bends over the back of the couch, spreading her legs wide. But before I fuck her, I want to kiss her neck and explore her skin. My lips find the tender flesh near her ear.

"You want this?" I ask her, my voice deeper than usual.

"Yes," she breathes.

I roll on the condom as I kiss her neck, dying to be inside her. "Fast or slow?" I ask as I skate my hand down her side, brushing her breast.

She shivers as I stroke her skin. "Fast. We don't have long."

I groan, wishing we could do this all night. The last thing I want to do is sit in a church and then a long-ass family dinner.

"We have forever, Mason," she says.

The words hit me.

We do have forever.

There are no more goodbyes.

"You're mine, Lizzy. Only mine."

"Only yours," she replies, her voice filled with conviction.

"Mine," I say again as I line up my cock and thrust inside her.

CHAPTER 20
LIZZY

"WHAT DO YOU THINK?" Zoey asks, turning around from staring at her reflection in the mirror. "Do I look okay?"

My vision blurs as my eyes fill with happy tears. "Stunning," I whisper, wishing my parents could be here for this day.

They would've loved seeing their only son getting married to the love of his life. Their absence has to be on Hunter's mind as much as it is on mine.

"Oh my goodness," Lulu squeals. "You're fucking beautiful, babe."

"Like a storybook," Tate adds.

The gown is the most beautiful wedding dress I've ever seen. I can see why Zoey lost her damn mind when they couldn't find it and she thought she'd have to wear something off the rack. Nothing would compare to the layers of lace and satin that fit her body like a glove.

The door to the bridal room opens, and Zoey's parents walk in. Her dad is the first to stop dead in his tracks as his gaze lands on his little girl.

"Baby," he whispers, his voice wavering like he's getting choked up. "You're so…"

"Beautiful," her mom breathes as she moves toward her daughter with tears streaming down her face.

I love Lucio and Delilah and the way they love their girls. Their gentle tenderness with each of them. Lucio doesn't hide his feelings or emotions, showering their daughters with compliments and hugs.

I use the moment to escape, needing a break. As soon as I am in the hallway, I press myself against the wall and melt into the cold stone. I've never been more thankful for a strapless dress in my entire life.

"Are you okay, darlin'?" a man asks in a deep voice.

Raising my gaze, I find a man I barely had time to speak to last night. "Pike, right?"

He nods. "You need help?"

"No. I'm good. I just needed a minute."

He leans against the wall next to me. "They can be a lot at first."

I smile and laugh softly. "They love each other so deeply."

"Shit parents?" he asks me, scratching at his beard.

"No, dead parents."

"Got that too, but mine were shit on top of it."

"I'm sorry," I say to him.

"The Gallos more than make up for it. Learn to embrace their over-the-top love, and you'll be fine."

"It's that easy?"

"It wasn't for me at first. Gigi's dad was also my boss. It made for an interesting start to our relationship."

"Really?" My mind reels with how that had to have worked. There's turmoil, and then there's *turmoil*. "That had to suck."

"Sometimes, but the family loved me, even though I came with a lot of baggage that followed me."

"Followed you?"

He shakes his head. "It's a story for another day."

Damn. I was hoping for a distraction, but Pike isn't willing to give me one. "I want to hear everything someday."

"Someday," he says as he pushes off the wall. "It's almost time. I'd better get back before Gigi comes looking for me."

"It was nice talking to you," I tell him as he straightens his suit. The man fills it out nicely too. He and Gigi are the type of couple that makes people stop dead in their tracks to admire their beauty. It's weird calling a man beautiful, but it's as if he stepped right out of a biker magazine cover shoot.

"You too. Enjoy today. It's a day to celebrate and soak in the Gallo goodness."

"I will," I tell him before I watch him walk away.

The door to the bridal room opens, and Delilah

walks out, dabbing her eyes with a tissue. "Lizzy," she says, her voice soft and wavering. "You look stunning in that dress."

"Thank you, Mrs. Gallo."

It's impossible not to gobble up their praise.

"You too," I add, because she's just a girl too, and who doesn't love a compliment.

"I need to take my seat. We're about to start."

That's my hint to get my ass inside to do final preparations before we walk down the aisle.

When I step back into the room, Mr. Gallo is at Zoey's side, holding her hands. "I love you, sweetheart," he tells her. "I wish you as much happiness as your mother and I have had for over thirty years."

My heart squeezes from the way he looks at her and the gentle sweetness of his words.

"Thanks, Daddy," she says to him.

He leans forward and kisses her cheek before releasing his hold on her hands. "We'd better line up."

Zoey's eyes move across the room, landing on me. "Lizzy, are you ready to be my sister?"

My body warms at the thought. "More than anything, babe."

A moment later, Amira comes bounding into the bridal room, dressed in the cutest soft-pink dress. "Auntie!" she screeches as she lunges for me.

I bend over to grab her before she has a chance to knock me off-balance, making this day a complete disaster. "Baby girl, don't you look adorable."

"Dad's getting married," she tells me, as if I don't know, but I can see the excitement on her face.

"He is."

Amira's gaze moves over my shoulder, and she gasps. "You look like a princess," she says to Zoey.

"Hey, sweetie. You look like a princess too," Zoey replies. "How's your daddy doing?"

"He's happy and can't stop moving," Amira says.

Hunter has to be nervous. It's not easy to have a roomful of people staring at you. I hate the idea of walking down the aisle today, but I know everyone will be looking at Zoey and barely paying attention to me. It's my one saving grace to stop a complete panic attack from taking over.

"You ready?" I ask my niece.

She gives a stiff nod. "Ready."

"Let's do this, people," Lulu says as she claps her hands. "It's showtime."

My belly rumbles as I set Amira back down on the floor. I concentrate on my breathing as I grab the bouquet, wrapping a strand of ribbon around my finger to give myself something to fiddle with when the nerves become too much.

Lulu arranges us in the order that we practiced last night at the entrance to the church. "The men are inside and will take your arm as soon as you walk through the door," she explains.

"We know, Lulu," Amelia groans. "We didn't forget since yesterday."

Lulu gives Amelia a look I can only describe as sour. "Thirty seconds," Lulu calls out before dashing to her spot in front of her sister—the matron of honor.

When the doors open and all the guests stand, my knees wobble. "Shit," I whisper and follow it with an apology because this isn't the place to let my mouth run wild.

Amira steps into the church, eating up the attention as she throws the flower petals wildly in the air. The people in the pews can't take their eyes off her, and I don't blame them. She's a cute little thing, even though she's growing bigger and older with each passing day.

Amelia's next to go, and Nino takes her arm, walking her down the aisle. Iris and Brax go next and then Tate and Wylder. I move forward, my body nearly shaking with nerves as I step toward the doorway, waiting for my cue to move.

But when I glance to the side, Mason's there. He's staring at me, smiling, and every bit of uncertainty vanishes. He moves into the doorway, taking my arm before I have a chance to take a step forward.

"I got you," he whispers.

No truer words. He's like an anchor for me. He tethers me to the earth at a time when my nervous energy is liable to cause me to float right off the ground.

"Hey," I whisper back.

"Hey, sweetheart."

I've never liked nicknames, but the softness of that word on his lips always makes me melt. I hope there's never a day when he stops using it when he talks to me. That'll be the day when I know the love is gone.

"Ready?" he asks as his brown eyes search mine.

"Ready," I tell him, and somehow my voice doesn't waver or crack.

This is my first time walking down an aisle. Somehow, I've escaped being a bridesmaid my entire life, and I'm not sad about it either. But today, in front of Mason's family, my steps feel sure and strong with him at my side.

The walk is quick before we peel apart, him going to his side of the church and me to mine. I should have my eyes focused on the back of the church and Zoey, but I can't stop staring at my guy. My future is across the aisle from me, and I hope someday we'll be here to celebrate our wedding in front of the same group of people.

Movement at the altar catches my attention, and I turn, finding my brother's gaze trained on the back of the church. Much like me, the very sight of his love makes his body calmer.

I've wanted this for him. I couldn't have picked a better woman to be his forever. Not only does he get a new family, but so do I.

We are no longer alone and never will be again.

CHAPTER 21
MASON

THE CHURCH WAS AS USUAL. A long ceremony, the exchanging of vows, and the end, which felt like it came hours later.

I curl my arm tighter around Lizzy and nuzzle my face into her neck as she sits in my lap at the reception. "Having fun?" I ask her, inhaling the soft lavender of her hair.

"Yes." She leans back against me, giving me better access to her neck.

The night has gone better than I'd hoped. Lizzy is relaxed and more comfortable around my family than she's ever been. She hasn't seemed overwhelmed, which would have been easy, given the number of people at the reception.

"How's the shop doing?" Gigi, my cousin from Florida and one of the owners of Inked near Tampa, asks my cousin.

Tate turns her champagne glass between her fingers as she stares across the table. "Better than ever. Business is booming."

"That's what I like to hear," Gigi replies as she leans over, resting against her husband. "You're doing great work with social media. It helps keep business steady, without all the expenses."

"Can we please talk about something other than work?" my cousin Tamara whines, rolling her eyes at their conversation.

Gigi straightens, glaring at our cousin. "Fine. What do *you* want to talk about?"

Tamara points a finger my way. "Them."

"Us?" I ask.

Tamara nods. "When did this start?"

"Here we go," Pike, Gigi's husband, mutters. "Always has to know everything."

"Zip it," Tamara tells him without looking his way. "I thought Mason would be a bachelor forever. So, I'm intrigued."

"There was a time when no one thought you'd ever settle down either," I remind her. Tamara wasn't known for her long-term relationships, and I never thought I'd see the day she'd become a mom.

Tamara pitches her thumb toward her very big husband. "It never would've happened without him."

"Well, duh," Gigi tells her, "You can't marry yourself."

"If I could've, I would've," Tamara tells her. "I wasn't looking for a relationship when I met him."

"No, you were looking for Crow," Mammoth, her husband, adds. "Thank God he had enough good sense to turn you away since he was going to prison."

"What?" I ask, never having heard this story before.

"Long story," Tamara mutters, waving her hand.

"No, it's not," her husband corrects her before lacing his fingers together and planting his grasped hands on the table in front of his impossibly large frame.

"I want to hear it," Lizzy says, leaning forward as if she's as invested in their story as I am.

I curl my arm tighter around her middle, holding her against me as we listen to Mammoth and get the dirt on my cousin's life before she became a mom.

"I was part of an MC back then."

"MC?" Lizzy asks.

"A motorcycle club. Tamara shows up at the compound, pounding on the door, and demands to see Crow."

"I didn't pound or demand anything," Tamara interrupts him.

"Princess, you did. Morris answered the door and told you to leave, but you wouldn't take no for an answer. Crow had to come to the door and tell you to kick rocks."

"So, how did you two get together, then?" Lizzy asks when Mammoth doesn't continue the story.

"I had to give her a ride."

"And that he did," Tamara says with a sinful smirk. "The rest is history."

I can't stop a bark of laughter from bubbling out of me. My cousin was always a wild one, but I don't think I realized the extent.

"You're missing a lot of bullets and danger along the way," Mammoth says.

"It's a family curse," Gigi explains. "Did anyone kidnap you yet, Lizzy?"

Even in the dim lighting of the reception hall, I can see Lizzy's face pale. "No. Why?"

"A lot of the Gallo women have been put in danger—and usually because of the men in our lives," Tamara explains.

"I didn't cause shit," Mammoth explains.

"Um, I disagree," Tamara argues, bumping him with her shoulder. "It was all worth it, though, because of how things ended."

Lizzy's hand moves to her collarbone as she stiffens. "Am I going to be kidnapped?"

I squeeze her gently. "Baby, I don't have any enemies. You're not going anywhere."

"Things are different here," Amelia tells our cousins from the South. "We don't get in trouble like you guys do down there."

Gigi raises an eyebrow. "Tate stepped in a giant pile of shit not too long ago. She spent some time in hiding with us in Florida."

"What?" I ask, not remembering anything about her life being in danger. "When?"

"It was years ago. It wasn't that big of a deal," Tate says, waving off the comment like we're not discussing her life.

"Really?" Pike asks, cocking his head to the side. "Seemed pretty big when you were down there."

"It was a long time ago. A stupid period in my life. And anyway, I fell in love with Inked when I was down there, and that's why I opened the tattoo shop here. It all worked out for the best in the end," Tate explains, leaning on the table with one elbow, a glass of champagne in her hand. "Can't stop fate."

"Is this fate?" Tamara asks, pointing at Lizzy and me again.

I nearly get whiplash from the change of topics with my family.

"I think it is," Tate answers for me. "If Hunter and Zoey hadn't met, then neither would they. It was meant to be. I could tell they fell for each other the second their eyes locked."

"Bullshit," I cough. "You couldn't tell anything by the look in my eyes."

Tate laughs. "Brother, I know you better than you know yourself. You were smitten with Lizzy immediately."

"That makes two of us," Lizzy says.

"You got me," I say, knowing my sister's right. As soon

as my eyes landed on Lizzy, I knew I wanted to be with her. It's as if there was an invisible rope that lassoed me to her, and I had no chance of escaping until I made her mine.

"Maybe we'll be sitting in this same spot for the two of you soon," Tamara says.

"Maybe," I reply, hugging Lizzy from behind.

Amelia drops down into the empty seat next to me and lets out a loud, exaggerated sigh.

"What's wrong?" Tate asks her because you'd have to be blind not to notice how upset Amelia is.

"I got stood up," Amelia says, glancing down at her hands in her lap.

"Fuck him, babe. Men are a dime a dozen," Tamara tells her.

"Ouch," I bite out.

"Not all men are assholes," Mammoth tells her.

Tamara rolls her eyes at her husband. "Ninety-nine percent aren't worth the time of day, baby. You know this."

"She ain't wrong," Pike adds. "Most are assholes."

"Present company excluded," Tamara adds.

"Of course," I mutter.

Tate takes Amelia's hand. "He's not the one, Amelia. Don't waste any more time thinking about him. Someday you'll find the one who would crawl across broken glass to spend time with you."

"That's a bit dramatic," Lulu says as she walks up behind Tate and places her hands on the back of her chair. "I don't think there's anyone I'd walk across broken glass for, let alone crawl."

"Your kids," Tate says without looking back at Lulu.

"Only them and, by extension, Oliver."

"Then that's not no one," Tate challenges her and then turns to Amelia. "See, when you really love someone, you'll do anything to see them."

Lizzy turns her head, her ass grinding against my cock underneath her weight. "Would you crawl across broken glass for me?"

I take her chin between my fingers and stare into her deep green eyes. "I'd crawl across broken glass or walk through fire to get to you, sweetheart."

"I love you," she says softly, but no amount of wedding music can hide the sound.

"I love you too," I tell her, leaning forward as I pull her face toward me. The world around us melts away as our lips meet, and we seal our declaration with a gentle kiss.

"You two are so cute," Tamara says, her voice cutting through our bubble of bliss. "To be young and in love again."

"Bitch, I'm not old. Speak for yourself," Gigi tells Tamara. "I'm still young and in love. Maybe you're an old hag here, but the rest of us are not."

"Lizzy's thirty-two," Amelia says.

Lizzy turns her head toward my cousin and nearly hisses, "That's not old."

"It's not young either," Amelia argues and laughs. "I'm kidding. Chill, girly pop."

"Girly pop?" I ask Amelia.

"I've been hanging out with Amira," Amelia says with a shrug.

"Sounds about right," I say.

"Kids," Amelia mutters. "I wish I could go back to those simpler times."

"Being an adult is way more fun," Lulu adds, "Anyway, I have a man to get to. Later." She waves before striding away.

Amelia stares at me so hard, I turn to her. "What?"

Her smile is sweet. "I never knew you were such a softy. I like this side of you," Amelia says. "Love suits you."

"Thank you," I tell her. "Don't settle for a douchebag, Amelia. If a man doesn't love you as deeply as I love this woman right here—" I squeeze Lizzy, and she nuzzles back into me "—then you walk away."

"That easy?" she asks.

"That easy," I tell her.

Zoey and Hunter stop at our table and stand behind Tamara and Mammoth. "Everyone doing okay?" Zoey asks, looking just as beautiful as she did earlier today. The hours of greeting guests and dancing haven't dulled the happiness that's radiating off her.

"We're great," Gigi tells her. "The wedding was beautiful. We're all so happy for you, Zo."

Zoey leans over and kisses Gigi's cheek. "I can't thank you all enough for coming up for the wedding."

"We wouldn't miss it," Tamara tells Zoey. "It's always nice to come back to our roots."

I wonder what life would've been like if their grandparents had stayed in Chicago. While I love going to Florida to see them, I would've rather had them around to hang out with when we were younger, and even now.

"The food is worth the trip alone, but spending time with everyone is the bonus," Tamara adds.

"Want to get out of here?" I ask Lizzy in her ear as I brush her hair over her bare shoulder with my fingers.

"And go where?"

"Quickie in the bathroom," I whisper to only her.

Lizzy chuckles. "We can't do that."

"Who says?"

Lizzy turns, her ass grinding against my dick again. "While it's tempting, it's almost time to cut the cake."

"There's only one thing I want to snack on."

Her eyes sparkle as she gazes at me. "You're so bad."

"That's not what it sounded like last night."

Lizzy's face turns a bright shade of pink. "Stop it."

"Who's ready for cake?" Zoey asks.

"Is it that time already?" Gigi asks.

"Time flies when you're having fun," Pike says.

"I love spending time with everyone. I think we need to buy a giant cabin in the mountains of Tennessee for us to all meet up and spend more time together. It's halfway for all of us," Gigi adds.

"I'd be down with that," Zoey tells her. "We'll have to talk about it another time, though."

"Of course. Just planting a seed," Gigi replies.

"Come on, sweetheart," Hunter says. "The cake awaits."

Lizzy pops off my lap and walks over to her brother. "I love you," she tells him before wrapping her arms around his body. "Thank you for this."

"For what?" he asks, staring down at his elder sister.

"For finding this family," she tells him. "We'll never be alone again."

I rarely thought about how lucky I've been to grow up with the Gallos. We are a large group, and never once in my life did I have to worry about being alone. No matter how much of a pain in the ass they are, I always have someone around when I need them. I've taken that for granted, but after meeting Lizzy and Hunter, I know how freaking lucky I've truly been.

EPILOGUE
LIZZY

ONE YEAR LATER…

ZOEY HOLDS up the onesie I scoured the internet to find. "Oh my God, this is so cute. Auntie's Girly Pop."

Amira wanted a matching one and wouldn't take no for an answer. "Amira helped me and now has one of her own."

"Amira wanted a onesie?" Zoey glances at Amira, who is giggling.

"No, Zo. My shirt says the same thing. See?" Amira lifts up her sweatshirt, showing Zoey her T-shirt underneath. "Now, Indigo and I can match."

Indigo. Something about that name makes me smile. I thought the baby looked more like an Ethel, but that's because she has the newborn wrinkles.

Mason takes my hand, giving it a squeeze. "Are you

doing okay?" he asks Zoey, concerned about his cousin. "Hunter told us the labor went long."

"Is there such a thing as a short labor?" Zoey asks, glancing up at my brother. "Was Amira fast?"

Hunter shakes his head. "She was long too."

"Maybe you're the problem," Zoey replies.

I chuckle, but I don't think she's wrong. "He's always been an issue, and I guess his sperm is too."

"What's sperm?" Amira asks, glancing between her father and me.

Hunter's face pales. "Um…"

"It's a seed," I tell her, keeping it as simple as I can, even though I'm very, very wrong.

"Does the stork drop it?" she asks.

"Yes," he tells her with a very quick nod.

"Oh. Okay," Amira says before she goes back to staring at her new little sister.

"Someday, I want one of those," Mason tells me, as if he's looking at a new piece of furniture.

"Those," I tell him, pointing at the sweetest little baby, "are a lot of work, and I'm getting too old to be pregnant."

"Bite your tongue, woman," he says. "We'd better get on it as soon as possible."

"Get on it?" Amira asks, always picking up on the shit she shouldn't.

"Ordering the seed," I tell her, covering for the innuendo.

"Order two so you can have two babies," Amira replies.

The very thought makes my stomach turn. I don't know how I'll handle one infant, let alone two. "That's a sweet thought, but I'd prefer one at a time."

"So, you're ready?" Mason asks.

"Shouldn't we get married first?" I ask him flippantly.

"Yes. Right away."

I gape at him, my mouth hanging open as I blink a few times. "What?"

"Right away," he repeats.

"Do it," Zoey says. "Amira and Indigo need a cousin."

"They have plenty of cousins," I tell her, because the family is already bursting at the seams.

Mason takes both my hands in his. "Let's do it. We'll elope. Go to Vegas and tie the knot."

"Eh. I don't love Vegas," I say.

"Where, then?"

"The Bahamas, on the beach."

"Sold," he says quickly. "I'll get it all booked, and we'll leave as soon as Zoey's back from maternity leave."

"Just the two of us," I tell him, because I want to have the honeymoon right after.

I have no reason to say no to him. Me from a few years ago would've had to plan everything, but

Mason's flipped my world upside down. I no longer need to be in charge all the time.

We've talked about marriage a few times, but never beyond casual conversation about it being a possibility in the future.

But like everything else with Mason, I jump in feet-first with very little thought. He is my future, and I know that deep in my bones.

"We're doing this." Mason leans forward and plants his lips on mine.

"I'm so happy." Zoey sniffles. "And these hormones are killing me."

"Hello," Tate says as she, Amelia, and Iris walk in. "We're here." But when Tate's eyes land on Zoey, she stops dead in her tracks. "Why are you crying?"

"They're getting married," Zoey says, but it's barely audible with her sobbing.

Iris's eyes shoot to us and widen. "You are?"

"Yep. In two months in the Bahamas."

"Oh, I love it there," Tate says. "I'll mark my calendar."

"Sorry, sis. This one is just for us," Mason tells her.

Tate's shoulders slump a little at his statement. "It's okay. It's not a good time anyway with the kids. It's harder and harder to get away lately."

Amelia takes a seat across the bed from us. She's unusually quiet, and I'm not the only one who notices.

"What's the face for?" Mason asks.

"What?" Amelia says, dragging her gaze across the bed to Mason.

"You look like someone broke your favorite toy," he explains.

"They kind of did," she whispers.

"What the hell does that mean?" Zoey asks her as she wipes her cheeks.

Amelia covers her face with her hands. "I think I'm pregnant."

———

Amelia's story continues in Promise. And it's one wild ride. Learn more and grab your copy at <u>menofinked.com/promise</u>

Want to read the first chapter of Promise? Turn the page.

———

PROMISE SNEAK PEEK

CHAPTER 1 - AMELIA GALLO

My parents are successful. And I don't mean they have good-paying jobs. They are well-known by everyone in our hometown and even around the world. My mother is a bestselling romance author, and my father was a professional football player for years. They gained their fame and success by the time they were my age, while I flit around, not knowing what to do with my life.

"Where are you?" my mother asks as I cover the bottom of my phone with my hand, trying to drown out the extremely loud music. "I can barely hear you."

"Out with Cassie. Some place near her house." I'm lying. Cassie's with me, but we're not near her house or even in the same state. "There's a band."

"Come on," Cassie whisper-shouts, pulling on my bare arm. "They're waiting." She glances over her shoulder at a group of guys who are looking at us like we're their next meal.

"I got to go, Mom. I'll call you tomorrow."

"You better," she says. "I love you."

"Love you too," I tell her before I hit end on my screen. "Are you sure about this?" Those words are for Cassie, but I don't know why I ask. I never trust her judgment.

"Yes, girl. Look at them." Cassie throws out her arm, making it perfectly clear we're talking about them.

Am I sure about this? Absolutely not. Are they hot as fuck? Absofuckinglutely yes! They look nothing like the guys back home. The three guys are over six feet tall, wearing old-school Levi's, snug T-shirts with rippling muscles on full display, and to top it all off, they're wearing cowboy hats.

"Where's Lyra?"

Cassie groans. "She's heading down the elevator now. She had to change. The girl has issues."

That statement is ripe coming from Cassie. The girl has more issues than any magazine ever printed.

"One night," I tell my friend, hoping it'll sate her need for attention from the opposite sex.

I agreed to come to Vegas for a girls' weekend and not to hook up with random men we'd never see again.

"Let your hair down, mama. You're wound tighter than a..." Cassie taps her lip. I can practically see her mind at work. The girl is not a wordsmith, never has been, but that's not why I love her.

"A yo-yo," I add, finishing her sentence.

She shakes her head, and her blond hair bounces in a way that makes me so damn jealous. "I was going to say banana."

It's my turn to groan. "That makes zero sense."

The elevator doors open, and Lyra steps out, glancing around until her gaze lands on us. She waves like we somehow didn't make eye contact. "I'm here. I'm here," she pants. "I had to run in these heels."

I look down as she points to her feet and wince. "Damn, Lyr. How the hell do you walk in those?"

Cassie and Lyra are glammed up, while I have on a pair of Chucks. Vegas is nothing but walking, and I'm not going to have my feet covered in blisters on the very first night and be miserable the rest of the trip.

Lyra lifts her foot, showing me the five-inch heels that are so skinny, I know I'd twist my ankle. "You know me, I was born in heels."

She's not even being dramatic. Her mother was a beauty queen, and from the moment Lyra could walk, her mother started to train her for the pageant life. The girl looks more awkward walking in flats than she does in stilettos.

"Are you two going to talk about shoes all night, or can we go ride some cowboys?" Cassie asks, tapping her left espadrille against the marble floor.

"Cowboys," Lyra nearly squeals. "I thought they were only in movies."

"Sweet Jesus," I mutter as Cassie and Lyra start to

move toward the three guys waiting about twenty feet away. I follow behind them, chewing on my bottom lip, hating every moment of this.

Part of me wants to run away and hide in my room with a good book. Add in a little room service, along with a bath, and it would be the perfect way to spend the evening. My room overlooks the strip, and while I've spent my life with big-city lights at night, Chicago's do not compare to Las Vegas.

"Howdy," the first cowboy says, taking off his hat and tipping his head.

So clichéd. They probably aren't even real cowboys. They probably wore the costume to snag women while on vacation—dumb ones like us. It's not any different from us getting dressed up and wearing heels when we spend most of our days in flip-flops.

"Hiya," Cassie says, her voice unusually high and more annoying. "I'm Cassie, and this is Lyra." She points at Lyra, who gives the guys a demure and completely fake smile. "And this is Amelia."

I give them a half-assed wave with zero enthusiasm. What in the actual hell have I gotten myself into?

The blond guy, who totally matches Cassie's vibe, gives her a big smile. "I'm Cliff."

Cassie does this weird little clap thing where the bottom of her palms stay touching but her fingers tap against each other. Is that supposed to be ladylike? It's kinda ew, but who am I to yuck her yum.

"And this is Dustin," Cliff says, pointing to the guy in a blue flannel he probably grabbed out of his hiking gear he hasn't touched in a year. "And that one is Reed."

When I drag my eyes to Reed, where Cliff is pointing, my heart stops dead in my chest. Reed is staring right at me, his eyes dark and dreamy with a hunger in his gaze that's slightly unnerving and more than a little hot.

Calm down, libido. He probably needs a steak.

"Dinner or drinks?" Cassie asks Cliff as she wraps herself around his arm, taking nothing slow.

"We've had dinner, but we'd be more than happy to watch you ladies eat," Cliff tells her.

"We've eaten too," she lies.

The only thing I had today was a bag of chips and the shitty dry-as-sand cookie they gave us on the plane. My stomach acid is about to start devouring me from the inside out if I don't get something in my system and soon.

"I'm hungry," I say, ignoring Cassie.

"I could eat," Reed adds with a tip of his head toward me. "How about we grab a table, and whoever wants to eat can eat and whoever wants to drink can drink."

"Fab idea," Cassie says, sounding every bit like a city girl and looking like one too with her bouncy hair, big tits, and long legs that go on for miles. There's nothing country about her, and maybe that's the allure for Cliff. He wants a taste of something outside his hometown, and that girl would be Cassie.

"Where to?" Reed asks.

I peer up, finding his eyes locked on me. "Um, I don't know. I've never been here."

"Who wants a steak?" Dustin asks. "They have a great one here."

There's no shock with his answer. These guys probably haven't eaten a vegetable in their lives besides a potato.

"You eat meat?" Reed asks me.

I nod. "I'm not an avocado toast kind of girl."

"Good," he says, his voice raking over my skin like a warm breeze. "Steak, it is." There's a slight twang to his words, but nothing that would scream he's from the South.

Reed holds out an arm for me to walk, and I take a step, expecting him to step behind me, but he doesn't. He stays at my side, slowing his stride so he doesn't pass me up. We follow Cassie, Dustin, Cliff, and Lyra and spend the first sixty seconds of the walk in silence.

Am I uncomfortable? A little, but growing up in a bar, I've become used to talking to strangers. And Reed, although handsome as hell, isn't different from any other man I've spoken to before.

"Where you from?" he asks.

"Chicago."

"Right on. I love it there."

I glance over at him, trying to picture him at Grant

Park with his hat on, looking completely out of place. "You've been?"

He nods. "My uncle lives in a place on Lakeshore. I used to spend a few weeks there every year when I was younger, but I don't go as much anymore."

There's nothing cheap on Lakeshore. I can't even afford a studio without a lake view in that area.

"Prettiest lake I've ever seen," Reed adds.

"It is that," I tell him, fiddling with the strap on my purse because this is so damn awkward. "And you?"

"I'm from Texas."

Of course he is. Do I believe he's a cowboy from Texas who vacations in Chicago? Not a fucking chance.

"What part?" I ask, pushing for more information.

"A little town called Hereford."

"Never heard of it."

"Like I said, it's a little place."

I make a mental note to do a bit of internet sleuthing later to find out all about his little hometown.

"You a rancher?" I ask, wanting more information.

"Yes, ma'am."

I ain't going to lie. The lilt to his words and the way he says ma'am have my heart doing a little dance behind my ribs.

"Five generations."

The Hook & Hustle is on its third generation. It's nowhere near as hard as ranching, but I know all about the ins and outs of a family business—the good, the bad, and the ugly.

"Amelia's family runs a business too," Lyra says as she turns around, totally eavesdropping on our conversation.

"Oh yeah?" Reed asks, somehow looking like he's interested, but I'm sure if I flashed him my tits, all thoughts about Lyra's statement would immediately disappear. "What kind?"

"A family bar."

"No shit," he says, staring down at me.

Standing next to the man makes me feel little. It's not something I'm used to either. My father is a large man, and so are most of the men in my family, but there's something about Reed that makes me feel smaller than normal.

"I don't work there. I work at my aunt's bakery next door," I say for no reason at all. I'm not embarrassed about the bar, but I want him to know that's not my life.

"I love dessert," he says.

I bet if I said I worked at the bar, he would've said he loved beer. Reed's trying too hard, when he doesn't have a shot at me, no matter what he says. I'm in my self-discovery era, and that doesn't include random hookups with strangers in different states.

I thank the gods as we turn a corner to walk into the restaurant, but my thanks doesn't last long. I nearly walk right into a giant cement bull that's three feet taller than me, and I stumble backward and screech.

Reed's hands shoot out lightning-fast, catching me by the arms. "Whoa," he says, capturing me in his grip as my eyes stare up at the ceiling with all my weight on my heels.

It all happened so damn quickly that if I had fallen completely backward, I know I'd be on my ass right now. With my luck, I would've broken something too.

My heart pounds inside my chest as I try to gather my thoughts about the entire clusterfuck of a situation. "Shit," I mutter as I find my footing and right myself. "Thanks."

"Anytime, darlin'," Reed says, but he doesn't release his hold on me. "You okay?"

"Embarrassed, but otherwise fine, thanks to you," I say and clear my throat, wishing the world would swallow me up whole.

"It's happened to me before, but with a real bull and a very different outcome," Reed says, trying to put my mind at ease. "Happens to the best of us."

"Sure," I whisper, glancing down to where our bodies are connected.

I don't hate it. His hands are warm and strong. The roughness of his skin tells me he does work outside and rarely uses gloves.

"Good thing you didn't have on heels. I think you would've gone over by the time I grabbed you."

"Yeah," I mumble.

Reed's hands drop away, and I immediately miss the contact. It's been ages since a man has touched me, but that's because the last one ruined penises for me for a very long time.

"Are you okay?" Cassie asks.

"I'm hungry," I tell her, wanting to forget about my near collision with the massive stone creature.

"Let's get you fed and off your feet," Reed says, taking my elbow and leading me toward the restaurant entrance.

My friends aren't the least bit fazed that I almost bit the dust. They're too interested in the men at their sides to pay any attention to me. I can't blame them. I am the clumsiest one out of the group, and what's my safety compared to the hunky cowboys on their arms.

Luckily, the restaurant isn't very crowded, and we don't need to wait for a table. It's relatively early for dinner in Vegas, but back home, it's already late. The time difference is doing me in, and tomorrow, I can guarantee I'll be awake before the sun peeks over the horizon.

The girls sit on one side and the guys on the other, with Reed sitting directly across from me. In between looking over the menu, I glance up at Reed and soak him in. I get my first full look when he takes off his hat and sets it in his lap.

He smiles at me, and I smile back. We're being very cordial as we both stare at the menu like it holds all the secrets to the universe.

The man is handsome. His face is tanned, with short stubble covering his jawline. I bet he could grow one hell of a beard if he didn't shave for a few weeks. And part of me wonders if it would be soft or if the hair would tickle the tips of my fingers. The hair on his head is dark with a slight wave, but it's cropped short in the back and longer on the top.

I drop my gaze back to the menu, not wanting him to catch me staring. There's steak and steak. Not much of a selection besides different cuts, but that's fine with me. I already know what I want.

"What are you getting?" he asks.

I bring my gaze back to him and meet his eyes. "Strip with mashed and sprouts."

"Mashed and sprouts?" He tilts his head like I'm speaking a foreign language.

"Mashed potatoes and brussels sprouts," I explain.

"Solid. I'm going for the Tomahawk and same sides."

"You like brussels sprouts?" God, I sound like an idiot even to my own ears.

"Yeah, darlin'. A man needs more than meat to survive. I like my veggies." He has tiny lines near his eyes when he smiles. Years of being in the sunshine have shown a little of his age, and I don't hate it. He looks grown compared to men my age back home, and it does things to my body it shouldn't. "But please tell me you aren't a well-done girlie."

I chuckle. There's something strange about him saying girlie. Cute, but weird. "I'm a medium-well girlie."

He sighs, rubbing his hand up and down his bare arm. "Not awful."

"Lemme guess," I say, straightening in my seat. "You're a rare kinda guy."

"No, beautiful. I like my meat cooked, but not overdone. I'm a solid medium."

I almost open my lips and tell him he's way above a medium, but somehow, I keep my mouth shut. Something I don't do very often. "I can do medium," I tell him instead, which doesn't sound much better.

His smirk tells me he takes those words just like they sounded, but not how I meant. "My kinda girl."

"Did you just buy that cowboy hat in the gift shop?" I tease him, wanting to change the trajectory of the conversation.

His dark eyebrows furrow, and fuck me, he looks adorable. "The gift shop?"

"Yeah."

He leans forward, placing his arms on the table. "What do you mean? You think I bought the hat here?"

I nod. "It's a good getup to snag the ladies."

"Did it snag you?" he asks, his head tilted as he studies my face.

"Almost."

"For your information, city girl, I brought this one from home, but it's the only one I brought with me."

"Why only the one?"

"It's black. It matches everything."

I laugh because he's not wrong. "How many do you own?"

He shrugs one shoulder. "Twenty."

"Twenty hats? That's so many."

"Some are old," he replies. "But you really think I bought this here and am lying about who I am?"

"Yeah, handsome. I do."

The waitress comes before he has a chance to respond. I can feel his stare as I place my order. I need alcohol, and I want it strong, but also sweet.

"Martini," he mutters before he turns his attention toward the waitress, who's waiting for his drink order. "Beer. Cold. Tall."

"Any specific beer?" she asks as her gaze moves around the male side of the table, noticing three very handsome men.

"Whatever you want. Surprise me."

"Got it," she says, moving on to the others at the table.

Reed reaches into his pocket and pulls out his phone. I watch him intently as he taps the screen.

"Hello," a woman's voice says from his hand.

"Ma. Go outside and show me the cows," he tells the woman. "I need to prove a point."

"Stop," I tell him, waving him off. "Leave the woman be."

"What in the hell are you doing there in Vegas, Reed? Show you the cows? I've never heard something so absurd."

I giggle but quickly cover my mouth in case she can hear me.

"Ma, please. Someone doesn't believe I live in Texas

on a ranch."

"Of all the dumb shit you've ever…" Her voice drifts off, and he stares at me, clearly wanting to show me how very wrong I am about him. "There."

Reed turns his phone around and shows me the screen. It's nothing but green and sunset skies, along with little dots of brown and black and a whole lot of moos. "Thanks, Ma."

"Who's that woman, Reed?"

"I'll call you tomorrow, Ma."

"She's purdy," she says, and something about the way she says it is so endearing to me. "Lasso yourself a wife while you're there."

Good thing I don't have my drink yet because I would've choked to death on her words.

"Ma. Stop. Not happening. Byeeeee," he says before tapping the screen and placing his phone face-side down. "Happy?"

"You didn't say you loved her before you hung up," I tell him.

"Don't need to repeat what she already knows. But you didn't answer. Still think I'm lying?" His eyes bore into me as he waits for my reply.

Foot meet mouth. "I believe you, cowboy."

"Good, darlin'. You think a city girl can outdrink a country boy?"

I swallow, remembering the last time I was shit-faced and how it took me days to recover. But I'm not one to shy away from a challenge, especially when it comes to drinking. You don't grow up in the bar life without having a certain inhuman threshold for liquor consumption. "I can, buddy. I'd put money on it."

"You're on, sweetheart. Challenge accepted," he says, and I immediately regret my answer when his eyes darken.

Shit.

———

Amelia's story continues in Promise. And it's one wild ride. Learn more and grab your copy at <u>menofinked.com/promise</u>

———

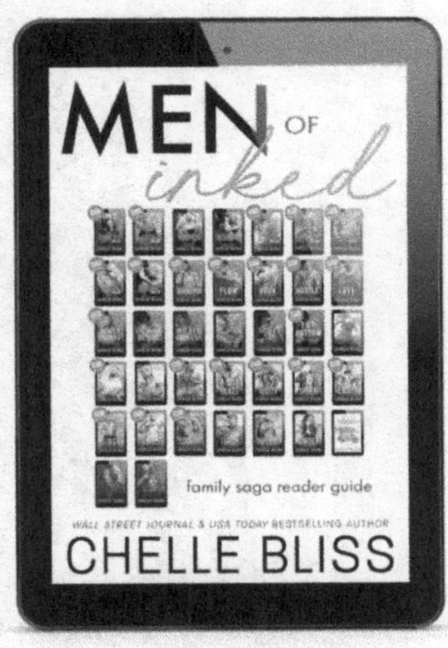

♥ Men of Inked Reader Guide ♥

DOWNLOAD NOW

Want more Gallos?

Tap here to get the Men of Inked Reader Guide, which includes a family tree, printable reading guide, and information about each Gallo family saga read.

The Men of Inked Southside series is also available in discreet paperback format for your enjoyment...

MEN OF *inked* MYSTERY BOX

DELIVERED EVERY THREE MONTHS

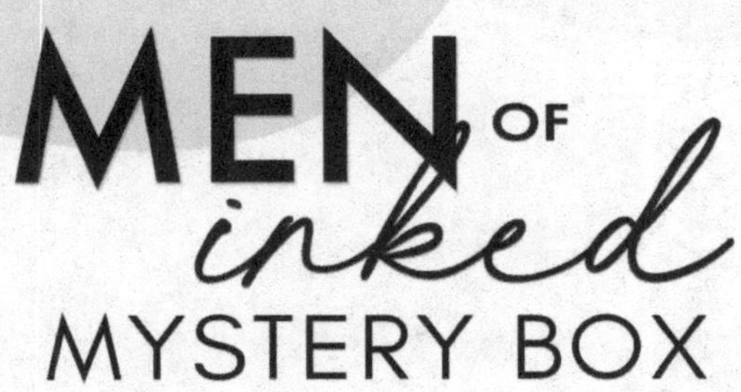

SPECIAL EDITION HARDCOVER & EXCLUSIVE MERCHANDISE!

CHELLEBLISSROMANCE.COM

BECOME A MEMBER OF THE FAMILY...

Want a place to talk romance books, meet other bookworms, and all things Men of Inked? Join Chelle Bliss Books on Facebook to get sneak peeks, exclusive news, and special giveaways.

Want to be the first to hear about the next Men of Inked book or everything Chelle Bliss? Join my newsletter by visiting *menofinked.com/inked-news* or scan the QR code below.

ABOUT THE AUTHOR

I'm a full-time writer, time-waster extraordinaire, social media addict, coffee fiend, and ex-history teacher. *To learn more about my books, please visit menofinked.com.*

Want to stay up-to-date on the newest Men of Inked release and more? <u>Tap here to join my newsletter</u> or visit *menofinked.com/inked-news*

Join over 10,000 readers on Facebook in <u>Chelle Bliss Books</u> private reader group and talk books and all things reading. <u>Tap here to become part of the family</u> or visit at *facebook.com/groups/blisshangout*

<u>Tap here to see the Gallo Family Tree</u> or visit *menofinked.com/gallo-family-tree*

Where to Follow Me:

facebook.com/authorchellebliss1

instagram.com/authorchellebliss

bookbub.com/authors/chelle-bliss

goodreads.com/chellebliss

amazon.com/author/chellebliss

tiktok.com/@chelleblissauthor

pinterest.com/chellebliss10

To purchase signed paperbacks and more, please visit

chelleblissromance.com